RAVES FOR

Me

FIVE YEARS FROM NOW

"Here's a recipe for personal growth: Take approximately equal parts of challenge, optimism, willingness, dedication and wisdom. Add a healthy measure of fun and sprinkle generously with delight. Season with time. Yield: ME: FIVE YEARS FROM NOW. How I wish I'd had this book five years ago. How glad I am to have it now!"

—**Kathleen Adams**
author of *Journal to the Self*

"Imagine a book devoted to you! Imagine opening a volume and finding out exactly what makes you tick! Imagine finding a book that encourages exactly the kind of changes you most want for yourself! Stop imagining it. It's here. ME: FIVE YEARS FROM NOW becomes your book with its thought-provoking questions and probing ideas."

—**Susan Kohl**
co-author of *Have a Love*
Affair with Your Husband
(Before Someone Else Does)

Produced by
The Stonesong Press, Inc.
Written by
Sheree Bykofsky

~ME~

F·I·V·E Y·E·A·R·S
F·R·O·M N·O·W

*A Planner for
Personal Growth and
Advancement*

WARNER BOOKS

A Warner Communications Company

Copyright © 1990 by The Stonesong Press, Inc.

All rights reserved
Warner Books, Inc., 666 Fifth Avenue, New York, NY 10103

A Warner Communications Company

Printed in the United States of America

First printing: March 1990
10 9 8 7 6 5 4 3 2 1

Created by The Stonesong Press, Inc. and
Written by Sheree Bykofsky

Book design by MaryJane DiMassi

ISBN 0-446-39097-6

Contents

PART IV: MY WORK AND SCHOOL

PART V: HERE I AM AGAIN:
BUILDING ON MY EXPERIENCE UP UNTIL NOW

The First Step:
How to Get the Most
From This Book

Most self-help books have one thing in common; they are somebody else's idea of what is good for someone like you. But is there really anyone else just like you? How far can we expect our powers of identification to extend?

Me: Five Years From Now is different because you are going to be the author. No one's name is on the cover or the title page because this book is yours. The approach and your questions were all written by me, Sheree Bykofsky, and the quotes which accompany them were selected and organized by me, but all of you who use this material will create your own script. You are best equipped to recognize the unique and distinct areas of your life that you want to change. You have your own set of problems and limitations. You have very special likes and dislikes and goals and dreams and plans. No one else in the world— not even your twin sibling—has the exact same group of family members and friends as you. This book is designed to become

*J*ust get it down on paper, and then we'll see
what to do with it.
—*Maxwell Perkins*

your personal tool. It can help you focus on yourself, examine your own particular sets of talents, possibilities, situations, limitations, and goals, and custom design your own future. To make it easy for you, there is room to write in the book, and it was designed so that you can open it, read from it, and rework your plans for at least the next five years—or even longer.

The key to planning, changing, and coping is to learn how to determine what important facets of your life you have control over and then to decide to exert that control in a positive way—one step at a time.

T·H·E B·A·S·I·C P·L·A·N: F·O·C·U·S, P·L·A·N, A·C·T, E·V·A·L·U·A·T·E

The formula for instituting change is really very simple:

First you need to *focus* on your situation, your problems, concerns, and needs. The Focus section will show you how to zero in on your likes and dislikes literally, by making two columns and writing them down. You will then examine your lists and decide what's important to you and what you have the ability to change.

Next, you will *plan* by, first, thinking about your options. You will work at keeping the good things and eliminating as many of the bad things as you can. What compromises are you willing to make? What are the risks?

*P*eople waste more time waiting for someone to take charge of their lives than they do in any other pursuit. Time is life. Time is all there is.
—*Gloria Steinem*

The third step is to *act*. This step will allow you to determine long- and short-term goals. You will think about what you can do today as a first step toward your long-term goals. Make up your mind to take at least one and up to three positive steps today toward achieving your goals. These can be little things, as simple as making an appointment, ordering a catalog, or changing the part in your hair. These are not chores. They are positive acts. They are part of the program that you have designed for yourself for the sole purpose of helping yourself.

The fourth step will be to *evaluate* your progress. This is done later, after you have embarked upon your plan. You will keep a record of what steps you have taken and all of the results—positive and negative. Then you can decide whether or not to chart a different course for yourself or continue as planned.

The book makes it easy for you to isolate different areas of your life so that you can focus on one set of plans at a time. Thus, it is divided into the following areas: Health, Relationships, Home, and Work. These larger areas are further subdivided into smaller areas. You may find, however, that you want to work on an area of your life that is not exactly touched on in this book. In that case, you can use this technique to work through virtually any problem, difficult decision, or plan. After you become familiar with the book, you will see that the core of the technique is the list that you yourself make. You can use it to cope with loss, decide whether or not to have a baby or get married, decide whether or not to buy a house, plan for retirement, or expand your business.

In a nutshell, all you need to do is list the positive on the left and the negative on the right, circle what's important, examine

*O*ptimism doesn't wait on facts. It deals with pros-
pects. Pessimism is a waste of time.
—*Norman Cousins*

your options, decide to change what you can, take action, and later evaluate. Take any situation; that is the idea.

For a brief example, here is how it might work for someone who has a business and is trying to come up with a five-year business plan. First she needs to ask herself a general question such as "what's my business like?" Then she needs to ask herself a series of specific questions. The answers should be written out in two lists, similar to the ones below:

Things I Like About My Business and Am Satisfied With	*Things I Don't Like About My Business and Would Like to Change*
I did better this year than last.	I'm not making as much $$ as I could.
I have two excellent employees.	Not everyone is pulling their weight.
I know more than the competition.	The competition is growing.
I have nice office space.	The office won't accommodate a growing business.
I'm making money on product x.	I'm losing money on product y.
My business has a personal touch.	I'm too generous with my time and people take advantage.
The post office is right across the street.	Certain people are prejudiced against women in this business.

The list could go on and on, but this is only a short example. Now the businessperson circles everything of importance on the list (which in this case is everything but the fact that the post office is right across the street).

The next step is to examine the list to figure out how bleak the picture really is and to determine what things are in the businessperson's power to change. In this case, she decides that the only thing she really has no control over is other people's prejudice. She decides that she does have the ability to improve several other areas of her business, though, and proceeds by making an "I could" list. Of all of the possibilities she comes up with, she thinks about which possible actions are too risky or would result in too many negative changes. One possibility that she abandons, for example, is to close up the business. She does decide, however, to do the following things: to replace a lazy employee; to discontinue product y and to promote product x; to hire an additional employee to screen phone calls; to do a market analysis; to mimic certain successful techniques of the competition; to seek larger office space in the same neighborhood, and so on. Many of these things take time, but the businessperson decides to do the following things today:

Send a warning to the offending employee.

Look through the classifieds to see what office space is going for.

Place an ad in the classifieds for a new employee.

*W*orry a little bit every day and in a lifetime you will lose a couple of years. If something is wrong, fix it if you can. But train yourself not to worry. Worry never fixes anything.
—Mary (Mrs. Ernest) Hemingway

*I*magination is the beginning of creation. You imagine
what you desire; you will what you imagine; and at
last you create what you will.
—George Bernard Shaw

Tomorrow the businessperson will come in an hour earlier. Next week's plan will be to interview prospective employees. Later she will evaluate the results of the changes. That's all there is to it.

You can control the direction of your life. The world is going to change around you, anyway. Why not exert a little positive control? All you have to do to make big things happen is to do a series of little things. And with a focus and a plan, it's easy and clear to do one or two small things each day if you know they have a purpose in the larger plan. For example, you might be intimidated by the idea of going back to school to improve your job. It may sound like too much. But if you've decided that it's a good idea, what's the harm of calling or writing a few schools and requesting their catalogs? When they arrive you can plan to look at them. If they appeal to you at that time, you can write for the applications and, perhaps, financial aid information. One thing at a time. That's all anyone can do. Still, the action is a step, and it keeps your mind on the goal you want to achieve.

Keep in mind, of course, that you don't have control over everything. You must assess your problems and plans and decide which things are in your complete or partial control to change and work on those. There are certain things you can't change: certain physical features and handicaps, most things about other

*I*f at first you do succeed—try to hide your astonishment.
—Harry F. Banks

people, your need for sleep; but you can change your attitude, your job, your religion, and your environment. You may not be able to change your friends, but you can change who your friends are. You may not be able to change your boss, but you can change your job or some of the problems associated with your job. You can't change your landlord (unless you have legal grounds) but you can move.

*T*he gift of fantasy has meant more to me than my talent for absorbing positive knowledge.
—*Albert Einstein*

The quotes in the book are here to encourage you and to remind you that although you are unique you are not alone. They also show that a sense of humor can be quite an asset. The long lists of questions and options provided in each section are just suggestions to get you started thinking about your life. They certainly won't apply to everyone and, in certain sections, you may prefer only to skim the questions or not even read them. That's fine; this is your book; you decide how to make it work for you.

Learning is enhanced by prior mental practice. If you can visualize a task before you do it, you will become proficient at the task faster than if you try to learn and do the task at the same time. Studies have shown, too, that people who imagine themselves as future successes have performed better than those who have imagined themselves as failures. If you imagine yourself as having achieved your goal, you will be more confident in going after it, are more likely to go after it, and you will be better equipped to handle whatever it is you have attained. You will also have the satisfaction of knowing that your plan worked; you achieved your goal. This is true in all areas of your life.

Moreover, people with goals—and especially people with written goals achieve much more than those with no goals. According to Forrest H. Patton, author of *Force of Persuasion*, "A study was made of alumni 10 years out of Harvard to find out how many were achieving their goals. An astounding 83 percent had no goals at all. Fourteen percent had specific goals, but they were not written down. Their average earnings were three times what those in the 83 percent group were earning. However, the three percent who had written goals were earning 10 times that of the 83 percent group."

Those who make an effort are successful—regardless of the results. If you've picked up this book and read this far, you're already on the road to improving your life over the next five years and beyond. Your next step is to pick an area that you would like to work on. Look for it in the table of contents. You will find that just as the different areas of your life overlap, so too will the table of contents. To really get the most from this book, you will use the many sections together. For example, if you are having trouble at work, perhaps you will turn first to Part IV, Chapter 1 (Work). After going through the chapter, you may find that one of the worst things about your job is getting along with a particular coworker or your boss. You may then decide to use the chapter of the book that zeros in on relationships, Part II, Chapter 5 (People I Must Deal With, Like It or Not). Many of the chapters work well with each other, such as Work and Financial Condition. You may wish to use the chapter Husbands and Wives to examine your relationship with your live-in lover, or you may wish to use the chapter for examining family relationships to examine a relationship with a friend who is "like family." You'll know best which chapter will prove most useful at any given time.

You may want to use a separate notebook to make very long lists so that sometime in the future you can rethink certain areas of your life and see how your outlook has changed. But this book was designed to be written in; after all, you are the author of your life.

I.

MY EMOTIONAL AND PHYSICAL HEALTH

1. Physical Condition and Health
2. Emotional and Psychological State
3. Religious and Spiritual Condition

1. Physical Condition and Health

F·O·C·U·S

Do I consider myself healthy or unhealthy and in good or bad physical condition?

This is my medical history:

_____

_____

_____

_____

_____

_____

_____

*W*hen we looked at the life cycle in our forties, we
looked to old people for wisdom. At eighty,
though, we look at other eighty-year-olds to see who got wise
and who not. Lots of old people don't get wise, but you
don't get wise unless you age.
—*Joan Erikson*

This is my current state of health: _____

_____

_____

_____

_____

_____

_____

_____

_____

   Make two lists side by side. On the left, list those things about
your health that you feel good about or satisfied with. On the
right, list the things about your health that trouble you. Think
of everything, general and specific, important and trivial, but
circle everything that is very important to you, because these
are the things that will deserve special attention later.
   Be sure to ask yourself any of the following questions that
apply to you. If you like, jot down your answers right on the
page. Then, later, transfer each answer to whichever list it fits;
it's possible that some things will go on both lists:

FOOD, WEIGHT, AND NUTRITION

Do I know what constitutes a healthy diet?

Do I eat a healthy diet?

What foods do I eat too much of?

What foods do I not eat enough of?

Do I overeat?

Do I undereat?

Do I have trouble losing/gaining weight?

What do I weigh and what would I like to weigh?

Do I feel healthy at my weight?

How do I feel after I eat?

GENERAL HEALTH AND HABITS

Do I take any medication on a regular basis?

Do I still need these medications?

Am I addicted to anything?

Do I have any specific medical complaints right now?

Do I suffer from any chronic ailments?

Am I satisfied with the medical care I get?

Do I see the doctor too frequently or not frequently enough?

Do I see other practitioners, such as chiropractors, acupuncturists, nutritionists, etc., and if so, how do I feel about my alternative practitioners?

When was the last time I had a checkup?

Am I honest with myself about my health?

Am I honest with others who inquire about my health?

What are my bad health habits?

What are my good health habits?

Do I have good hygiene habits?

Have I successfully broken any bad habits?

Have I tried unsuccessfully to break any bad habits?

Have I stopped pursuing my good habits?

Do I take care of my teeth?

How is my eyesight?

How is my hearing?

Do I suffer from frequent colds or other common ailments?

Do I pay too much attention to my health?

Do I pay enough attention to my health?

Do I feel I'm aging well?

*Y*ou don't stop laughing because you grow old; you grow old because you stop laughing.
—Michael Pritchard

EXERCISE

How is my energy level?

Am I able or better able to do most things that healthy people of my age can do?

What kind of exercise do I get?

Is exercise important to me?

Do I get enough exercise?

Do I enjoy my exercises?

Does exercise make me feel healthier?

What are my physical limitations?

Do I wish I could do things I used to be able to do?

Am I prevented from doing these things because I am "out of shape" or as a natural consequence of aging or because of some other physical limitation?

Do I have any physical limitations that prevent me from achieving my health goals, and if so, what are they?

APPEARANCE

Do I like my body?

What do I like best about my appearance?

What things about my appearance bother me?

Do I pay too much or not enough attention to my body?

Do I sacrifice my health for the sake of my appearance? If so, how?

Do I sacrifice my health for any other reason (i.e., no time to floss my teeth, too expensive to visit the doctor, no health coverage)? If so, is it worth the sacrifice?

HEALTH PROGRAMS

Do I enjoy taking care of my health or do I feel it's a bother?

What are five other specific things about my health that I like and don't like?

Am I on the road to good health?

Do I do anything good for myself and my body on a regular basis (massage, facial, pedicure, manicure, reflexology, etc.)?

Are my current health programs and habits long term or short term?

Do I want to be following the same programs and habits in five years?

Realistically, how do I see myself in terms of my health one year from now and five years from now?

Is my present course taking me there?

What other issues regarding my health do I want to explore?

Today my heart beated 103,389 times, my blood traveled 168,000 miles, I breathed 23,040 times, I inhaled 438 cubic feet of air, I spoke 4,800 words, I moved 750 major muscles, and I exercised 7,000,000 brain cells.
I'm tired.
—Bob Hope

Things I Like About My Physical Health	*Things I Don't Like About My Physical Health*

List as many things as possible.

A *man begins cutting his wisdom teeth the first time he bites off more than he can chew.*
—Herb Caen

Now that you've made two lists, it's time to examine them. First of all, which is longer? Which is longer when you consider only those items that are circled (the things that are important to you)?

If the list of important things you don't like is much longer than the list of things you do like, you might then consider asking yourself whether or not you are really taking care of your health in a satisfactory manner. If the list of things you do like is much longer, you might then consider emphasizing maintenance over the next five years. In either case, it's time to work on changing whichever circled items are within your control to change.

So that's the next important question to ask yourself: Which items on the list of things I don't like are within my control to change? (It may help to examine the reasons these problems exist in the first place.)

P·L·A·N

What are three things I can do to change each item on the list? List everything now. Later go back and think about the consequences and repercussions of each possible action. Think then, for example, if rectifying a problem will negatively affect any of the things on the other list, the things you do like about your health.

*D*o one thing . . . imagine . . . see it and live it.
Don't think it up laboriously, as if you were
working out mental arithmetic. Just look at it, touch it,
smell it, listen to it, turn yourself into it.
—Ted Hughes

THINGS I CAN CHANGE ABOUT MY PHYSICAL HEALTH

A.

B.

WAYS TO CHANGE THEM

A 1.

2.

3.

B 1.

2.

3.

I was thinking, forty five—that's middle age. Well, I'm going to have the best damn middle age anybody ever had.
—*Laura Z. Hobson*

POSSIBLE CONSEQUENCES

A 1.

   2.

   3.

B 1.

   2.

   3.

Following is a list of general and specific positive actions you may want to consider taking. Not everything on the list of suggestions will apply to you nor will they all be right for you. It is hoped, though, that the list will inspire you to come up with your own ideas about how to help yourself, plan for the future, and improve your life. Not forgetting to weigh the risks and consequences, could you see yourself taking any of these actions?

FOOD, WEIGHT, AND NUTRITION

I could join a weight reduction program.

I could eat a more balanced diet.

I could eat smaller portions.

I could eat more slowly.

I could lose/gain _____ pounds.

I could start bringing my lunch to work.

I could start eating breakfast.

I could have more fiber, more vegetables, less fat, less sugar, more fruit, less processed food, less salt, less coffee, more protein, less cholesterol, less soda, less alcohol, etc.

I could get off of this unhealthy diet.

I could read a book about dieting.

I could try some new recipes.

I could join a food co-op.

I could go to a farmer's market.

GENERAL HEALTH AND HABITS

I could get a checkup.

I could see a specialist.

I could ask my friends to recommend doctors.

I could look into health coverage.

I could get information about surgery.

I could make an appointment with the dentist.

I could see a hypnotist.

I could see a chiropractor.

I could see a nutritionist.

I could get a massage.

I could do what the doctor recommended.

I could get a second opinion.

I could take a vacation.

I could try to relax.

I could stop smoking.

EXERCISE

I could use the local health club.

I could start doing the exercises that my health permits.

I could exercise longer.

I could walk more.

I could walk up stairs instead of taking the elevator.

I could jog.

I could do yoga.

I could exercise with a friend.

I could ride a bicycle.

I could combine activities, such as reading and exercising.

I could set aside a half hour a day to _____ .

I could swim more often.

I could learn a new sport.

I could play the sport I am good at more often.

I could call my friends and arrange to play a game.

I could dance.

I could join a dance or aerobic or weight-training class.

I could make an appointment with a personal trainer.

I could buy a new pair of sneakers.

I could get or use my exercise apparatus.

I could join a team (bowling, basketball, softball, etc.).

APPEARANCE

I could consider some cosmetic changes.

I could look into cosmetic surgery.

I could wear more flattering clothes.

I could get a manicure or give myself one.

I could take better care of my ⎯⎯⎯⎯⎯⎯⎯⎯⎯ .

I could get a new haircut.

I could use a depilatory or get electrolysis.

I could shave my moustache or grow a beard.

I could buy a new perfume or cologne.

I could dye my hair.

I could vacation at a spa.

I could try a facial mask.

I could wear a hat or hairpiece.

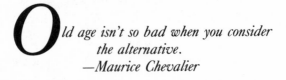

*O*ld age isn't so bad when you consider
the alternative.
—*Maurice Chevalier*

I could use cosmetics.

I could stop using cosmetics.

I could get contact lenses or new glasses.

HEALTH PROGRAMS

I could ask people who have been successful how they did it.

I could ask my friend to stop tempting me with _____ .

I could get counseling for my _____ addiction.

I could read a book about natural cures.

I could ask the doctor to recommend programs to help with my bad habits.

I could do a work-out video or TV work-out program.

I could try to locate an expert by asking people, by looking in the Yellow Pages, by researching at the library.

I could set aside more time for _____ .

I will try to accept the fact that I'm _____ .

I could stop _____ .

I could stop _____ .

I could start _____ .

I could start _____ .

I could _____ .

I could _____ .

I could _____ .

Now it's time to . . .

A·C·T

Look at your new list and ask yourself the following questions:

Which of these things could I do or start doing today?

Which of these things take time?

Are there any first steps I can take today to achieve any of my long-term goals? (For example, if you've decided that you may want to join a health club, today you could call a few or visit one.)

What are the general things I will try to do?

Tell yourself, I will do at least one new thing per day until I am satisfied with the state of my physical health. I will do everything in my power to work within my limitations. I will try to set realistic goals and will note each accomplishment. I will perceive myself as successful just for trying, and I will be gentle with myself if things do not turn out the way I expect. If I do not accomplish something I have set out to do, I will consider the possibility that I have tried to change something that is not within my power to change, and I will try to learn lessons that

*I*f you're not failing now and again, it's a sign
you're playing it safe.
—*Woody Allen*

will help me in this and other areas of my life. I will not expect to change everything all at once but will take things one step at a time.

Things I Could Do Today:	*Things That Take Time:*

I Will Do the Following Things Today:

2. Emotional and Psychological State

F·O·C·U·S

The part of my life that causes me the most stress is:

My Emotional and Physical Health (Part I)
My Family and Relationships (Part II)
My Home and Community (Part III)
My Work and School (Part IV)
Other
I Don't Know
Everything

If you answered "everything," instead of continuing, you may wish to consider seeking professional assistance. Continue in this section if your answer is "other" or "I don't know." Otherwise, go to the appropriate section in the book.

If I were describing myself in the third person as a character in a novel, this is what I would say:

This is how I'd like to be remembered when I'm gone:

This is how I think the person who knows me best would describe me:

Which is the more accurate description of me?

How would I like to change that person's perception of me?

How would most people describe me?

What would I like to change about that description?

*H*ow *many cares one loses when one decides not to be*
something, but to be someone.
—*Gabrielle ("Coco") Chanel*

Make two lists side by side. On the left, list everything about yourself and your way of living that you like and that make you feel good. On the right, list everything about yourself and your way of life that you don't like and that make you feel bad. Think of everything, general and specific, important and trivial, but circle everything that is very important to you, because these are the things that will deserve special attention later.

Ask yourself any or all of the following questions that apply to you. If you like, jot down your answers right on the page. Then, later, transfer each answer to whichever list it fits; it's possible that some things will go on both lists:

My favorite time of day is _____.

My most productive time of day is _____.

When I wake up in the morning I usually feel _____.

When I _____ I feel great.

When I _____ I feel great.

After I _____ I feel great.

After I _____ I feel great.

When I _____ I feel terrible.

When I _____ I feel terrible.

After I _____ I feel terrible.

After I _____ I feel terrible.

Some things that persistently trouble me are _____ .

*D*on't put off for tomorrow what you can do today, because if you enjoy it today you can do it again tomorrow.
—*James Michener*

Things I keep doing that I dislike doing are ——————— .

Do I have a positive or a negative self-image?

What do I like best about myself?

What do I like least about myself?

My best talents are ————————————— .

I haven't had success at ————————————— .

I wish I could ————————————— .

I should face the fact that I'm no good at ——————— .

People tell me I should change my ————————— .

I get the most compliments on my ————————— .

I would like to get the most compliments on my ——————— .

Do I like myself?

Do other people like me?

Do I like to help other people or do I tend to hurt them?

Do I feel basically understood or misunderstood?

Am I good at communicating my feelings?

Do I care what people think of me?

S elf-pity in its early stages is as snug as a feather mattress. Only when it hardens does it become uncomfortable.
—Maya Angelou

*O*ur life always expresses the result of our
dominant thoughts.
—*Soren Kierkegaard*

One character trait I would like to develop is ——————.

One character trait I would like to try to rid myself of
is ——————————————.

Do I need more fun in my life?

What do I need more of in my life?

Do I usually know what's bothering me?

Do I think I'm always capable of figuring it out?

Do I wish I understood myself better?

Am I too emotional?

Am I not emotional enough?

Do I cry too much or not enough?

Do I worry too much?

Do I sleep well at night?

Do I feel guilty about things?

Do I blame myself for many things?

Am I too careful or reckless?

Am I too anything?

Do my emotions often get out of control?

Do I lose my temper too easily?

Do I display my emotions appropriately?

Am I often afraid?

Am I often confused?

How do I generally deal with my problems?

Do my methods or philosophies for dealing with my problems generally work for me?

Can I handle my own problems: never, usually, or always?

Am I afraid to get help, and if so, why?

What things am I particularly proud of?

What are the things in my life that make me happiest?

What things about myself make me happiest?

Realistically, how do I see myself in terms of my emotional health one year from now and five years from now?

Is my present course taking me there?

What other issues concerning my emotional health do I want to explore?

*I*f a person is to get the meaning of life he must learn to like the facts about himself—ugly as they may seem to his sentimental vanity—before he can learn the truth behind the facts. And the truth is never ugly.
—Eugene O'Neill

Things I Like About Myself and My Emotional Health	*Things I Don't Like About Myself and My Emotional Health*

List as many things as possible.

*I*f you really know what things you want out of life, it's amazing
how opportunities will come to enable you to carry them out.
—John M. Goddard

Now that you've made two lists, it's time to examine them. First of all, which is longer? Which is longer when you consider only those items that are circled (the things that are important to you)?

If the list of important things you don't like is much longer than the list of things you do like, you might then consider asking yourself whether or not you are really taking care of your emotional health in a satisfactory manner. If the list of things you do like is much longer, you might then consider emphasizing maintenance over the next five years. In either case, it's time to work on changing whichever circled items that are within your control to change.

So that's the next important question to ask yourself: Which items on the list of things I don't like are within my control to change? (It may help to examine the reasons these problems exist in the first place.) Remember that it is hard or impossible to change other people, but even though there are limitations and risks, you do have at least some control to change yourself and your life. And do not lose sight of those things about your life that are important for you to keep.

P·L·A·N

What are three things I can do to change each item on the list? List everything now. Later go back and think about the consequences and repercussions of each possible action. Think then,

I take a simple view of living. It is keep your eyes open and get on with it.
—Laurence Olivier

for example, if rectifying a problem will negatively affect any of the things on the other list, the things you do like about your life.

THINGS I CAN CHANGE ABOUT MYSELF

A.

B.

WAYS TO CHANGE THEM

A 1.

   2.

   3.

B 1.

   2.

   3.

To know oneself, one should assert oneself.
—Albert Camus

POSSIBLE CONSEQUENCES

A 1.

   2.

   3.

B 1.

   2.

   3.

Following is a list of general and specific positive actions you may want to consider taking. Not everything on the list of suggestions will apply to you nor will they all be right for you. It is hoped, though, that the list will inspire you to come up with your own ideas about how to help yourself, plan for the future, and improve your life. Not forgetting to weigh the risks and consequences, could you see yourself taking any of these actions?

I could try to be more patient.

I could try to be more persistent.

I could try to be calmer.

I could try to be more assertive.

I could be a better listener.

I could choose friends who are more supportive of me.

I could listen to my friends more when they tell me truths about myself.

I could stop closing myself off to people.

I could let my friends and family help me more.

I could be more _____ .

I could be less _____ .

I could keep being _____ .

I could get help from _____ to
stop _____ .

I could get help from _____ to
start _____ .

I could ask my friends what they like best about me.

I could ask them what they like least about me.

I could practice _____ .

I could _____ more often.

I could _____ less often.

I could read a self-help book.

I could watch _____ .

I could get up earlier or later in the morning.

I could go to bed earlier or later at night.

I could relax by _____ .

I could change my _____ .

I could keep my _____ .

I could stop pretending to _____ .

I could try to understand my feelings about _____ .

I could get help trying to understand my feelings about _____ .

I could write down my dreams.

I could keep a journal.

I could write to _____ .

I could call _____ .

I could be a better _____ .

I could admit to _____ .

I could talk to _____ .

I could insist on _____ .

I could visit _____ .

I could stop trying to please _____ .

I could start trying to please _____ .

I could start _____ .

I could start _____ .

I could stop _____ .

I could stop _____ .

I could _____ .

I could _____ .

I could _____ .

Now it's time to . . .

A·C·T

Look at your new list and ask yourself the following questions:

Which of these things could I do or start doing today?

Which of these things take time?

Are there any first steps I can take today to achieve any of my long-term goals? (For example, if you've decided that you want to be more tolerant of someone else's values, today you could go to the library and get the book that he or she recommended to you years ago or you could call him or her.)

What are the general things I will try to do?

Tell yourself, I will do at least one new thing per day until I am satisfied with the state of my emotional health. I will do everything in my power to work within my limitations. I will try to set realistic goals and will note each accomplishment. I will perceive myself as successful just for trying, and I will be gentle with myself if things do not turn out the way I expect. If I do not accomplish something I have set out to do, I will consider the possibility that I have tried to change something that is not within my power to change, and I will try to learn lessons that will help me in this and other areas of my life. I will not expect to change everything all at once but will take things one step at a time.

41

Things I Could Do Today:	*Things That Take Time:*

I Will Do the Following Things Today:

*T*here are only two ways to live your life. One is as
though nothing is a miracle. The other is as though
everything is a miracle.
—*Albert Einstein*

3. Religious and Spiritual Condition

F·O·C·U·S

Is spirituality an important concept for me? If yes, how do I celebrate my spirituality? How do I think of myself in terms of religion and spirituality?

Make two lists side by side. On the left, list all of those things about your religious and spiritual condition that you feel good about or are satisfied with. On the right, list all of the things about it that trouble you. Think of everything, general and specific, important and trivial, but circle everything that is very important to you, because these are the things that will deserve special attention later.

Be sure to ask yourself any of the following questions that apply to you. If you like, jot down your answers right on the page. Then, later, transfer each answer to whichever list it fits; it's possible that some answers will go on both lists:

Do I practice, observe, or commemorate my spirituality as often or as much as I would like to?

Do I practice what I believe?

If spirituality isn't a concern of mine, am I comfortable and guilt-free about this?

Can I explain my beliefs to family or friends who don't agree with my view or who are more or less spiritual?

Do I care to explain?

Do I believe in God?

What, if any, is my conception of God?

Do I believe in a being higher than myself?

Do I believe in an afterlife?

Is this something I think or care about?

Am I concerned about death?

Do my religious beliefs help me deal with fears, problems, questions, or important issues in my life?

Is there anything else that helps me cope with life?

Is "faith" an important concept to me?

Do I have a spiritual or religious role model?

Do I admire any others with opposing views? If so, how do I reconcile this?

Where do I think spirituality comes from (born with it, taught, parents, God, books, etc.)?

Has my concept of God changed over the years? If so, do I prefer my old concept or my new concept?

Is my concept of God a more traditional image, or is it altogether different?

Do I wish I believed in God?

Do I believe that people have the ability to decide their religious beliefs?

Do I believe that my religious beliefs are a condition of my cultural tradition?

Am I currently having a religious crisis?

How am I dealing with it?

Do I want other people to think the way I do? If so, everyone else or just the people I love? Why?

Do I insist that others believe what I believe? Why or why not?

If I have children, or if I plan to have children now or someday, do I (plan to) pass on my religious views to them?

How do (will) I feel if they spurn my views?

Can I change their views?

Would I be happier if I reconsidered my position or if I stuck with it?

Would my children be happier if I reconsidered my position?

Does the question of marriage between people of different religions affect my life? If so, how?

Would I be happier if I reconsidered my opinion?

What would be the result if I changed my opinion?

Would others be happier if I reconsidered?

What would be the result for them if I did?

Have I been influenced by anyone who insisted that I believe what he/she believed? If so, what benefits and drawbacks have resulted?

Have I ever been angered by anyone who insisted I believe what he/she believed, and why?

How do I reconcile the fact that I want to influence others, but I don't want them to influence me (if that's the case)?

How do my religious views help me or hurt me?

Do I want to change my religious views and, if so, how?

Do I believe that change is something within my control?

How would I be better off?

Would religion help everybody? If so, any particular religion?

Do I think that some religions are better than others or that some people are better than others because of their religion?

Do I discriminate against anyone because of their religious views? If so, how do I explain that?

What things about my religion should I or must I accept?

Are there other ways to cope with my problems besides turning to religion?

Would I be better off turning to religion or to a new religious practice to cope with my problems?

Are there other things about my religion that make me particularly happy, comfortable, calm, or satisfied?

Are there other things about my religion that make me particularly sad, confused, or nervous?

Realistically, how do I see myself in terms of my religion and spirituality one year from now and five years from now?

Is my present course taking me there?

What other issues concerning my spiritual condition do I want to explore?

Things About My Religion and Spirituality That I'm Happy or Satisfied With	*Things About My Religion and Spirituality That I'm Not Happy or Satisfied With*

List as many things as possible.

*T*here can be blessings in the most painful of experiences, even at the vortex of a scandal or the breakup of a marriage. In the midst of the turmoil, everything looks bad. Helpful friends may assure you that it's always darkest before the dawn, but when you're living with pain, optimism seems impossible. Yet everyone needs and deserves these assurances, because the assurances are true. Even the most horrible experience can be big with blessings.
—John Ehrlichman

Now that you've made two lists, it's time to examine them. First of all, which is longer? Which is longer when you consider only those items that are circled (the things that are important to you)?

If the list of important things you don't like is much longer than the list of things you do like, you might then consider asking yourself whether or not you are really attending to your spiritual and religious needs in a satisfactory manner. If the list of things you do like is much longer, you might then consider emphasizing maintenance over the next five years. In either case, it's time to work on changing whichever circled items that are within your control to change. It's in this section that the question of control for many people becomes particularly difficult to determine. What you yourself believe is ultimately the most important consideration here.

But that's the next important question to ask yourself: Which items on the list of things I don't like are within my control to change? (It may help to examine the reasons these problems exist in the first place.)

P·L·A·N

What are three things I can do to change each item on the list? List everything now. Later go back and think about the consequences and repercussions of each possible action. Think then,

*Y*ou can have anything you want if you want it desperately enough. You must want it with an inner exuberance that erupts through the skin and joins the energy that created the world.
—Sheilah Graham

for example, if rectifying a problem will negatively affect any of the things on the other list, the things you do like about your spirituality.

THINGS I CAN CHANGE ABOUT MY RELIGION AND SPIRITUALITY

A.

B.

WAYS TO CHANGE THEM

A 1.

  2.

  3.

B 1.

  2.

  3.

*G*od grant me the serenity to accept the things I cannot
change, the courage to change the things I can,
and the wisdom to know the difference.
—Reinhold Niebuhr

POSSIBLE CONSEQUENCES

A 1.

   2.

   3.

B 1.

   2.

   3.

Following is a list of general and specific positive actions you may want to consider taking. Not everything on the list of suggestions will apply to you nor will they all be right for you. It is hoped, though, that the list will inspire you to come up with your own ideas about how to help yourself, plan for the future, and improve your life. Not forgetting to weigh the risks and consequences, could you see yourself taking any of these actions?

I could seek or speak to a religious or spiritual advisor.

I could seek a new religious or spiritual advisor.

I could read the Bible or other religious books appropriate to my specific religion of choice.

I could read books other than those pertaining to my specific religion.

I could take a class.

I could learn about various other religions.

I could visit an ashram, convent, synagogue, mosque, temple, school, or other religious institution or place of worship.

I could speak to a friend that I trust.

I could work on solving my problems through another outlet (such as psychotherapy, meditation, weekend seminar, encounter group, support group, discussion group, etc.).

I could go to my place of worship more often.

I could become more involved in the activities of my place of worship.

I could stop going to my place of worship.

I could travel to ancient sacred sites (such as Greece, India, Jerusalem, the Vatican, my ancestors' home, etc.).

I could examine the source of my beliefs.

I could examine the source of my problems.

I could examine how my religion is helping me and others.

I could examine how my religion is hurting me and others.

I could make an effort to help others.

I could be more charitable.

I could do community service.

I could try to support my spouse's, children's, or other loved ones' views.

I could try to understand their way of thinking.

I could teach my children what I believe and tell them why.

I could send my children for religious training.

I could expose my children to other religions.

I could expose myself to other religions.

I could celebrate more than one religion.

I could modify my religion by ———————————— .

I could try to be more tolerant.

I could participate in religious holidays.

I could sit on the beach at sunset to meditate.

I could convert.

I could pray.

I could stop ———————————————— .

I could start ——————————————— .

I could ————————————————— .

I could ————————————————— .

Now it's time to . . .

A·C·T

Look at your new list and ask yourself the following questions:

Which of these things could I do or start doing today?

Which of these things take time?

I don't think of all the misery, but of the beauty that still remains. . . . My advice is: Go outside, to the fields, enjoy nature and the sunshine, go out and try to recapture happiness in yourself and in God. Think of all the beauty that's still left in and around you and be happy!
—*Anne Frank*

Are there any first steps I can take today to achieve any of my long-term goals? (For example, if you've decided that you want to learn more about your religion, today you could visit your local place of worship to find out about what classes they offer.)

What are the general things I will try to do?

Tell yourself, I will do at least one new thing per day until I am satisfied with my religious and spiritual condition. I will do everything in my power to work within my limitations. I will try to set realistic goals and will note each accomplishment. I will perceive myself as successful just for trying, and I will be gentle with myself if things do not turn out the way I expect. If I do not accomplish something I have set out to do, I will consider the possibility that I have tried to change something that is not within my power to change, and I will try to learn lessons that will help me in this and other areas of my life. I will not expect to change everything all at once but will take things one step at a time.

Things I Could Do Today: | *Things That Take Time:*

I Will Do the Following Things Today:

*T*he truth that many people never understand, until it
is too late, is that the more you try to avoid suffering
the more you suffer because smaller and more insignificant
things begin to torture you in proportion to your
fear of being hurt.
—*Thomas Merton*

E·V·A·L·U·A·T·E

I will keep a list here of all of the things I've done and the results I've achieved:

DATE	STEP TAKEN	RESULTS

II.

MY FAMILY AND RELATIONSHIPS

*1. Parents, Siblings, Children,
and Other Relatives
2. Husbands and Wives
3. Boyfriends, Girlfriends, and Lovers
4. Friends
5. People I Must Deal With, Like It or Not*

1. Parents, Siblings, Children, and Other Relatives

NOTE: FOR EACH OF THE SECTIONS IN THIS CHAPTER, IT WILL BE HELPFUL TO CONCENTRATE ON ONE PERSON AT A TIME.

F·O·C·U·S

Think of one of your parents, a sibling, your child, or other relative whose relationship with yourself you wish to examine or improve. Describe that person as if he or she were a character in a novel.

Now in general terms, describe your relationship with that person:

*T*he most important thing a father can do for his children is to love their mother.
—*Theodore M. Hesburgh*

Make two lists side by side. On the left, list all of the things about that relationship that you are happy or satisfied with. On the right, list all of the things about that relationship that trouble you or which you would like to improve. Think of everything, general and specific, important and trivial, but circle everything that is very important to you, because these are the things that will deserve special attention later.

Ask yourself any of the following questions that apply to you. If you like, jot down your answers right on the page. Then, later, transfer each answer to whichever list it fits; it's possible that some things will go on both lists:

When I think about this person, what are the major feelings that come to mind?

Are those feelings recent, or deep-rooted?

Is this a person I care about very much?

Is this a person who cares for me very much?

How much influence has this person exerted over my life?

In what ways has this person influenced my life?

Overall, has this person had a positive or negative influence?

Do I love this person?

Why do I think I love this person?

Did this person have to earn my love?

What are the qualities I like best in this person?

What are the qualities I like best about our relationship?

Do I feel our relationship entitles me to anything from this person, and if so, what?

What do I hope to derive from our relationship?

Do I derive those things?

Would I say our relationship is equal or one-sided?

Who puts more into our relationship, me or this person?

Is this relationship one of my priorities?

Does this relationship take a lot of time away from other relationships or priorities?

Do I want to put more into the relationship?

Do I wish he/she put more into the relationship?

How important do I think I am to this person?

How would I change this person if I could?

How do I think this person would change me if he/she could?

Am I willing to change myself to please this person?

Do I care about pleasing this person?

Do I feel I owe this person anything, and if so, what?

Do I live with this person, and if so, is that a good thing for me?

Also, do I expect different things from this person because I live with him/her?

Do I respect and look up to this person?

Does this person respect and look up to me?

Does he/she rely on me, and if so, is it too much or not enough?

What are the problems with this relationship that have always bothered me?

What are the problems that have only begun to bother me recently?

Has our relationship changed for the better, for the worse, or has our relationship not changed too much over the years?

In what ways has our relationship changed over the years?

If this person weren't related to me, would I be his/her friend?

Does my relative do things that bother me?

Do I think those things are done on purpose?

Does this person care if he/she annoys me?

Do I annoy this person? If so, do I annoy this person deliberately?

Do I think this person is justified in being annoyed?

Does this person help me in any general way?

What are some specific ways this person has helped me?

Have I helped him/her?

Do I feel comfortable talking to this person?

Are there subjects I deliberately avoid talking to this person about, and if so, why?

When I think about it, are those reasons valid?

Are we fairly open with each other?

Is it important for me to be intimate with this person?

Are we intimate?

Is this person interested enough in my problems?

Does this person pry too much or overly disturb my privacy?

Do I respect his/her privacy?

If I could tell this person anything in the world, what would it be?

Have I already told him/her? If no, why not?

Could I tell him/her now?

Did it or would it change anything, and if so, for the better or the worse?

Does this person listen when I talk to him/her?

Does he/she remember the important things I tell him/her?

Does this person respond in a way that satisfies me?

Do I listen well to what this person has to say?

Do I remember things he/she tells me?

Do I respond in a way that satisfies this person?

Do we share many or very few of the same opinions?

Do we argue very much?

Are those arguments enjoyable or troublesome?

Do we fight fair or "hit below the belt"?

Do we always argue about the same things, and if so, what?

Do we raise our voices, more or less than we do with other people?

Has this person hurt me in any great way?

Was it deliberate or did he/she have good intentions?

If I could put myself in this person's shoes, how would I describe his/her reason for hurting me?

Can I forgive him/her?

Has this person tried to make it up to me?

Have I hurt this person in any great way?

Did I hurt him/her deliberately or did I have good intentions or was it just an accident or side-effect?

Am I sorry and, if so, have I tried to make it up to him/her?

Did this person forgive me?

Do I forgive myself?

Do I see or talk to this person as much as I would like to?

Do I see or talk to this person too much?

When was the last time we hugged or kissed?

What things do I hate about this person?

Have I told him/her?

Could I tell him/her?

Have we worked through the bad feelings?

If this person were no longer in my life, would I be sad or happy?

What would I miss?

What would I be glad about?

What would I be sorry I didn't tell him/her?

What would I be glad I didn't tell him/her?

If someone else could replace the role this person plays in my life, who would I choose?

What qualities does that other person have that my relative lacks?

What qualities does my relative have which that other person lacks?

Do I want this person to nurture me?

Do I want to be nurtured by this person? In what ways?

Does this person make me feel good or bad about myself?

Do I think this person understands me better or worse than other people?

Does this person restrict me in anyway, and if so, in what ways?

Do the restrictions make sense to me?

Do I think that this person has a good reason for imposing those restrictions?

What reason does he/she give?

Does this person open up new possibilities for me, and if so, what?

Would I say that this person is good or bad to me?

Would I say that this person is good or bad for me?

*M*y father died many years ago, and yet when something special happens to me, I talk to him secretly not really knowing whether he hears, but it makes me feel better to half believe it.
—Natasha Josefowitz

I looked on child rearing not only as a work of love and duty but as a profession that was fully as interesting and challenging as any honorable profession in the world, and one that demanded the best that I could bring to it.
—Rose Kennedy

Am I good to and good for this person?

Am I dependent upon this person or is this person dependent upon me? In what ways?

Do I like to be alone with this person?

In what situations do I enjoy this person most?

What things do we enjoy doing together most?

Can I pinpoint any jealousies that trouble me?

Can I pinpoint any other feelings of guilt, secrets, or hostilities in my family?

Is family important to me?

What are the most important things about family to me?

Would I say my family is generally close or distant?

Do I contribute to that?

Realistically, how do I see myself in terms of my family relationships one year from now and five years from now?

Is my present course taking me there?

What other issues concerning my family relationships do I want to explore?

Good Things About My Family Relationship(s)	*Bad Things About My Family Relationship(s)*

List as many things as possible.

*I*f you expect perfection from people, your whole life is a
series of disappointments, grumblings, and complaints.
If, on the contrary, you pitch your expectations low, taking
folks as the inefficient creatures which they are, you are
frequently surprised by having them perform better
than you had hoped.
—Bruce Barton

Now that you've made two lists, examine them. First of all, which is longer? Which is longer when you consider only those items that are circled (the things that are important to you)?

It's unlikely you can change your family, but you can work on changing whichever circled items that are within your control to change. So that's the next important question to ask yourself: Which items on the list of things I don't like are within my control to change? (It may help to examine the reasons these problems exist in the first place.)

P·L·A·N

What are three things I can do to change each item on my list? List everything now. Later go back and think about the consequences and repercussions of each possible action. Think then, for example, if rectifying a problem will negatively affect any of the things on the other list, the things you do like about your relationship.

THINGS I CAN CHANGE

A.

B.

WAYS TO CHANGE THEM

A 1.

   2.

   3.

B 1.

   2.

   3.

POSSIBLE CONSEQUENCES

A 1.

   2.

   3.

B 1.

   2.

   3.

Following is a list of general and specific positive actions you may want to consider taking. Not everything on the list of suggestions will apply to you nor will they all be right for you. It is hoped, though, that the list will inspire you to come up with your own ideas about how to help yourself, plan for the future, and improve your life. Not forgetting to weigh the risks and consequences, could you see yourself taking any of these actions?

I could try to do more for this person.

I could buy this person a gift.

I could send this person a card.

I could invite him/her over for lunch or dinner.

I could ask him/her for an invitation.

I could tell him/her what I've always wanted to say.

I could ask this person to be honest with me.

I could try to listen better to what he/she tells me.

I could ask for his/her side of the story.

I could spend more or less time with him/her.

I could confide in this person more/less.

I could suggest we do something together.

I could suggest we stop doing something that causes us trouble.

I could try to change the way I do something.

I could try to change the way we do something.

I could try to be more independent.

I could be more/less demanding.

I could encourage this person to be more/less dependent upon me.

I could help this person with a problem.

I could do more to help this person in general.

I could ask this person to help me.

I could inform this person of my problem.

I could let bygones be bygones.

I could forgive this person.

I could forgive myself.

I could try to get help for dealing with my guilt, jealousy, or anger.

I could try to get out of the house more.

I could spend more time at home.

I could move in with this person.

I could move out.

I could make more quality time to see this person.

I could stop taking this person for granted.

I could improve the quality of our relationship by _____ .

I could ask this person to _____ .

I could ask this person to stop _____ .

I could put an end to an unhealthy factor in our relationship.

I could hug this person.

---

*B*eing a housewife and a mother is the biggest job in the world, but if it doesn't interest you, don't do it. . . . I would have made a terrible mother.
—*Katharine Hepburn*

I could tell this person that I love him/her.

I could suggest we go for family therapy.

I could go for therapy alone.

I could set aside more time for _____.

I could try to accept the fact that this person is and will always be _____.

I could stop _____.

I could stop _____.

I could stop _____.

I could stop _____.

I could start _____.

I could start _____.

I could start _____.

I could start _____.

I could _____.

I could _____.

I could _____.

I could _____.

I could _____.

I could _____.

I could _____.

I could _____.

73

Now it's time to . . .

A·C·T

Look at your new list and ask yourself the following questions:

Which of these things could I do or start doing today?

Which of these things take time?

Are there any first steps I can take today to achieve any of my long-term goals? (For example, if you've decided to spend more time together, today you could start making arrangements to make it happen.)

What are the things I will try to do in general?

Tell yourself, I will do at least one new thing per day until I am satisfied with the state of my relationship(s). I will do everything in my power to work within my limitations. I will try to set realistic goals and will note each accomplishment. I will perceive myself as successful just for trying, and I will be gentle with myself if things do not turn out the way I expect. If I do not accomplish something I have set out to do, I will consider the possibility that I have tried to change something that is not within my power to change, and I will try to learn lessons that will help me in this and other areas of my life. I will not expect to change everything all at once but will take things one step at a time.

Things I Could Do Today:	*Things That Take Time:*

I Will Do the Following Things Today:

2. Husbands and Wives

F·O·C·U·S

Describe your spouse as if he or she were a character in a novel.

Now in general terms, describe your relationship with your spouse:

Make two lists side by side. On the left, list all of those things

about your relationship with your spouse that you are happy or satisfied with. On the right, list all of the things about your relationship that trouble you or which you would like to improve. Think of everything, general and specific, important and trivial, but circle everything that is very important to you, because these are the things that will deserve special attention later.

Ask yourself any of the following questions that apply to you. If you like, jot down your answers right on the page. Then, later, transfer each answer to whichever list it fits; it's possible that some things will go on both lists:

When I think about my spouse, what are the major feelings that come to mind?

Are those feelings recent, or deep-rooted?

If recent, what precipitated the recent feelings?

Do I care for my spouse more than anyone in the world?

Whom do I care for more?

If I had it to do over today, would I marry my spouse?

What attracted me to my spouse initially?

Do those things still attract me?

What developed over time?

Is my spouse my best friend?

*L*earn how to pay compliments. Start with the members of your family, and you will find it will become easier later in life to compliment others. It's a great asset.
—Letitia Baldridge

Are we tolerant of each other's needs?

Am I easy to live with, and why?

Is my spouse easy to live with, and why?

Do we respect each other's privacy?

Do we take each other for granted?

In what ways has my spouse influenced my life?

Overall, has my spouse been a positive or negative influence?

Do I love my spouse very much?

Does my spouse love me very much?

What do I love most about my spouse?

What are the qualities I like best in my spouse?

What are the things I like best about our marriage?

What do I expect to obtain from our marriage?

Do I get those things?

Did I used to get those things?

Would I say our relationship is equal or one-sided?

Who puts more into our relationship, me or my spouse?

Do I want to put more into the marriage?

Do I wish he/she would put more into the marriage?

Do we share the housework?

Who does more of the housework?

Do we have similar standards of cleanliness?

Have we worked out our finances in a way that is satisfactory to us both?

Does one of us have more control over important decisions than the other?

Are we both happy with these arrangements?

How is our relationship like that of our parents?

How is it different?

Which similarities and differences am I happy about and which am I sorry about?

Do we get along with each other's family?

Is this a source of conflict?

How important do I think I am to my spouse?

How would I change my spouse if I could?

How do I think my spouse would change me if he/she could?

How would I change our relationship if I could?

Am I willing to change myself to please my spouse?

Do I care about pleasing my spouse?

Do I feel I owe my spouse anything, and if so, what?

Do I expect different things from my spouse than I do from other people?

Do I think my spouse expects too much from me?

Do I respect and look up to my spouse?

Does my spouse respect and look up to me?

Does he/she rely on me, and if so, is it too much or not enough?

What are the problems with our relationship that have always bothered me?

What are the problems which have only begun to bother me recently?

In what ways has our relationship changed over the years?

Has our relationship changed for the better, for the worse, or has our relationship not changed too much over the years?

Does my spouse do things that bother me?

Do I think those things are done on purpose?

Does my spouse care if he/she annoys me?

Do I annoy my spouse? If so, do I annoy my spouse deliberately?

Do I think he/she is justified in being annoyed?

Does my spouse help me in any general way?

What are some specific ways my spouse has helped me?

Have I helped my spouse?

Do I feel comfortable talking to my spouse?

Are there subjects I deliberately avoid talking to him/her about, and if so, why?

When I think about it, are those reasons valid?

Are we fairly open with each other?

Does our sex life satisfy me?

How would I like to change it?

Are we as intimate as I would like to be?

Is my spouse interested enough in my problems?

Does my spouse pry too much or overly disturb my privacy?

Do I respect his/her privacy?

If I could tell my spouse anything in the world, what would it be?

Have I already told him/her? If no, why not?

Could I tell him/her now?

Did it or would it change anything, and if so, for the better or the worse?

Does my spouse listen when I talk to him/her?

Does he/she remember the important things I tell him/her?

Does he/she respond in a way that satisfies me?

Do I listen well to what my spouse has to say?

Do I remember things he/she tells me?

Do I respond in a way that satisfies my spouse?

Do we share many or very few of the same opinions?

Do we argue very much?

Are those arguments enjoyable or troublesome?

Do we fight fair or "hit below the belt"?

Does my spouse or do I use physical force when we fight?

Do we always argue about the same things, and if so, what?

Do we raise our voices, more or less than we do with other people?

Has my spouse hurt me in any great way? If so, was it deliberate or did he/she have good intentions?

If I could put myself in my spouse's shoes, how would I describe his/her reason for hurting me?

Can I forgive my spouse?

Has he/she tried to make it up to me?

Have I hurt my spouse in any great way?

Did I hurt my spouse deliberately or did I have good intentions or was it just an accident or side-effect?

Am I sorry and, if so, have I tried to make it up to my spouse?

Does my spouse forgive me?

Do I forgive myself?

Do I see my spouse as much as I would like to?

Do I spend too much time with my spouse?

When was the last time we hugged or kissed?

What things do I hate about my spouse?

Have I told my spouse?

Could I tell him/her?

Have I worked through the bad feelings?

If my spouse were no longer in my life, would I be sad or happy?

What would I miss?

Whenever you want to marry someone, go have lunch with his ex-wife.
—*Shelley Winters*

What would I be glad about?

What would I be sorry I didn't tell him/her?

What would I be glad I didn't tell him/her?

Have I ever met anyone else I think I could have been happy being married to?

If marriage was a possibility, why didn't I marry that person?

Possible or not, what qualities did or does that other person have that my spouse lacks?

What qualities does my spouse have which that person lacks?

Do I want to be nurtured by my spouse?

In what ways?

Do I want to nurture my spouse?

Does my spouse make me feel good or bad about myself?

Do I think my spouse understands me better or worse than other people?

Does my spouse restrict me in anyway, and if so, in what ways?

Do the restrictions make sense to me?

Do I think my spouse has a good reason for imposing those restrictions?

*T*o escape criticism—do nothing, say nothing, be nothing.
—*Elbert Hubbard*

What reason does my spouse give?

Does my spouse open up new possibilities for me, and if so, what?

Would I say my spouse is good or bad to me?

Would I say my spouse is good or bad for me?

Am I good to and good for my spouse?

Am I dependent upon my spouse or is my spouse dependent upon me?

In what ways?

Do I like to be alone with my spouse?

In what situations do I enjoy my spouse most?

What things do we enjoy doing together most?

Do we have enough separate interests, involvements, and friends to keep us happy?

Do we have enough common interests, involvements, and friends to keep us happy?

Is this a source of conflict?

Do I always/usually/rarely prefer to spend my time with my spouse?

How much time would be just right?

Do we have enough fun together?

Am I jealous of my spouse?

Is my spouse jealous of me?

Can I pinpoint any feelings of guilt or hostility that come between us?

What other aspects of my marriage would I like to deal with or change?

Does this relationship take a lot away from other relationships or priorities, such as those with my parents or children?

Do I have or want to have children?

How does my spouse feel about having children?

Do we agree about how to rear children?

Do I put myself first, my spouse first, or my children first?

Who would I like to put first?

Who do I think I ought to put first?

Are there issues associated with children that come between us?

What are the most important things about marriage to me?

Do I derive or do I anticipate deriving those things from our marriage?

Some other problems my spouse and I need to resolve
are _____ .

Realistically, how do I see myself in terms of my marriage one year from now and five years from now?

Is my present course taking me there?

What other issues concerning my marriage do I want to explore?

Things I Like About My Spouse and My Marriage	*Things I Don't Like About My Spouse and My Marriage*

List as many things as possible.

Now that you've made two lists, examine them. First of all, which is longer? Which is longer when you consider only those items that are circled (the things that are important to you)?

In either case, it's time to work on changing whichever circled items that are within your control to change. So that's the next important question to ask yourself: Which items on the list of things I don't like are within my control to change? (It may help to examine the reasons these problems exist in the first place.)

P·L·A·N

What are three things I can do to change each item on the list? List everything now. Later go back and think about the consequences and repercussions of each possible action. Think then, for example, if rectifying a problem will negatively affect any of the things on the other list, the things you do like about your marriage.

THINGS I CAN CHANGE

A.

B.

WAYS TO CHANGE THEM

A 1.

   2.

   3.

B 1.

   2.

   3.

POSSIBLE CONSEQUENCES

A 1.

   2.

   3.

B 1.

   2.

   3.

Following is a list of general and specific positive actions you may want to consider taking. Not everything on the list of suggestions will apply to you nor will they all be right for you. It is hoped, though, that the list will inspire you to come up with your own ideas about how to help yourself, plan for the future, and improve your life. Not forgetting to weigh the risks and consequences, could you see yourself taking any of these actions?

I could try to do more for my spouse.

I could buy my spouse a gift.

I could send my spouse a card.

I could tell my spouse what I've always wanted to say.

I could ask my spouse to be honest with me.

I could try to listen better to what he/she tells me.

I could ask for his/her side of the story.

I could spend more or less time with him/her.

I could try to improve the quality of our time together.

I could tell my spouse how I spent my day.

I could confide in my spouse more/less.

I could suggest we do something together.

I could suggest we stop doing something that causes us trouble.

I could try to change the way I do something.

I could try to change the way we do something.

I could try to be more independent.

I could be more/less demanding.

I could encourage my spouse to be more/less dependent upon me.

I could help my spouse with a problem.

I could do more to help my spouse in general.

I could ask my spouse to help me.

I could inform my spouse of my problem.

I could let bygones be bygones.

I could forgive my spouse.

I could forgive myself.

I could try to get help for dealing with my guilt, jealousy, or anger.

I could try to get out of the house more.

I could spend more time at home.

I could hire a housekeeper or baby-sitter.

I could insist we distribute our money in a fairer way.

I could insist we distribute the housework or other responsibilities in a fairer way.

I could stop flirting with other people.

I could insist my spouse stop flirting with other people.

I could insist we do more as a family.

I could suggest that we swap some of our established roles or chores.

I could improve the quality of our relationship by _____ .

I could ask my spouse to _____ .

I could ask my spouse to stop _____ .

I could hug my spouse.

I could tell my spouse that I love him/her.

I could wear something sexy to bed.

I could get satin sheets.

I could do something I know my spouse will like.

I could offer to do something for my spouse that I know will make him/her happy.

I could do something that I know he/she has always wanted me to do.

I could ask him/her to do something for me.

We could take a course together.

We could take a course in massage together.

We could give each other massages.

We could do something romantic.

We could try to develop a new mutual hobby.

We could plan a vacation together.

I could set aside more time for _____.

I could read a book about improving our sex life.

I could insist that we share more responsibilities around the home.

I could suggest we go for couples counseling.

No problem is so big or so complicated that it can't be run away from.
—Linus, Peanuts *cartoon character*

I could suggest we separate.

I could demand a divorce.

I could get a lawyer.

I could try to accept the fact that my spouse is and will always be _____ .

I could stop _____ .

I could stop _____ .

I could start _____ .

I could start _____ .

I could start _____ .

I could start _____ .

I could _____ .

I could _____ .

I could _____ .

I could _____ .

I could _____ .

We could _____ .

We could _____ .

We could _____ .

We could _____ .

We could _____ .

Now it's time to . . .

A·C·T

Look at your new list and ask yourself the following questions:

Which of these things could I do or start doing today?

Which of these things take time?

Are there any first steps I can take today to achieve any of my long-term goals? (For example, if you've decided to take a vacation together, today you could call a travel agent.)

What are the things I will try to do in general?

Tell yourself, I will do at least one new thing per day until I am satisfied with the state of my marriage. I will do everything in my power to work within my limitations. I will try to set realistic goals and will note each accomplishment. I will perceive myself as successful just for trying, and I will be gentle with myself if things do not turn out the way I expect. If I do not accomplish something I have set out to do, I will consider the possibility that I have tried to change something that is not within my power to change, and I will try to learn lessons that will help me in this and other areas of my life. I will not expect to change everything all at once but will take things one step at a time.

Things I Could Do Today:	Things That Take Time:
_____	_____
_____	_____
_____	_____
_____	_____
_____	_____
_____	_____
_____	_____
_____	_____
_____	_____

I Will Do the Following Things Today:

_____

_____

_____

_____

T he greatest thing in family life is to take a hint when a hint
is intended—and not to take a hint when a hint
isn't intended.
—Robert Frost

3. Boyfriends, Girlfriends, and Lovers

F·O·C·U·S

Describe your ideal boy/girlfriend:

If you have one, describe your boy/girlfriend as if he or she were a character in a novel and make comparisons with your ideal (if you have several, just think about one at a time):

Now in general terms, describe your relationship with your boy/girlfriend:

Make two lists side by side. On the left, list all of those things about your love life and your relationship with your boy/girlfriend(s) that you are happy or satisfied with. On the right, list all of the things about your love life that trouble you or that you would like to improve. If you have more than one boy/girlfriend, deal with only one at a time. You may use these questions to examine a relationship that is over; just think about the questions in the past tense. Think of everything, general and specific, important and trivial, but circle everything that is very important to you, because these are the things that will deserve special attention later.

Ask yourself any of the following questions that apply to you. If you like, jot down your answers right on the page. Then, later, transfer each answer to whichever list it fits; it's possible that some things will go on both lists:

3A: IF YOU DON'T HAVE A BOY/GIRLFRIEND

Is it by choice that I don't have a boy/girlfriend?

Why do I think I do not have a boy/girlfriend?

What's good about not having a boy/girlfriend?

What's bad about not having a boy/girlfriend?

Can I make the bad things good in ways that don't involve having a boy/girlfriend?

Do I prefer to be alone or with people?

Am I comfortable meeting new people?

Do I put myself in situations that make it difficult or easy to meet new people?

Do I have a specific idea about the kind of person I would like to go out with?

Have I ever met such a person?

Have I met many people whom I would like to go out with?

Were there reasons I couldn't ask them out?

Was I or am I afraid of being rejected, and why?

Is there any way that I could meet more people?

Do I have friends that could introduce me?

Do I have friends that are good at meeting people?

Do they do things that I wish I could do?

Is it possible that I could do some of those things?

What qualities do I have that they may wish they had?

Are there any clubs I might consider joining?

Is there anything about having a boy/girlfriend that frightens me?

Is there anything about not having a boy/girlfriend that frightens me?

Do I expect that I will just meet someone someday, or do I think I will have to make it happen?

3B: IF YOU HAVE ONE OR MORE BOY/GIRLFRIENDS

When I think about my boy/girlfriend, what are the major feelings that come to mind?

Are those feelings recent or have I felt them for a long time?

Have I felt those feelings with or for anyone else?

If recent, what precipitated the recent feelings?

Do I care for my boy/girlfriend more than anyone in the world?

Whom do I care for more?

Would I consider marrying my boy/girlfriend and why or why not?

Do I think our relationship is too serious or not serious enough?

Do I wish I could stop seeing this person?

Am I hoping this relationship will lead to marriage?

Do I think about or care about getting married?

What do I think marriage to this person would be like?

What attracted me to my boy/girlfriend initially?

Do those things still attract me?

What feelings developed over time?

Is my boy/girlfriend my best friend?

Are we tolerant of each other's needs?

In what ways has my boy/girlfriend influenced my life?

Overall, has my boy/girlfriend been a positive or negative influence?

Do I love my boy/girlfriend? Why or why not?

Do I think my boy/girlfriend loves me?

Have we told each other?

What are the qualities I like best in my boy/girlfriend?

What do I like best about our relationship?

Do I expect anything from my boy/girlfriend that he/she gives me?

Do I expect anything from my boy/girlfriend that he/she denies me?

Did I used to get those things?

Would I say our relationship is equal or one-sided?

Who puts more into our relationship, me or my boy/girlfriend?

Do I want to put more into the relationship?

Do I wish he/she would put more into the relationship?

Do we share good things with each other?

Do we share the costs and responsibilities in a way that pleases us both?

Does one of us have more control in making decisions than the other?

Are we both happy with these arrangements?

Do we get along with each other's family?

Do we get along with each other's friends?

Is this a source of conflict?

How important do I think I am to my boy/girlfriend?

How would I change my boy/girlfriend if I could?

*T*rouble is part of your life, and if you don't share it, you don't give the person who loves you a chance to love you enough.
—Dinah Shore

How would I change our relationship if I could?

How do I think my boy/girlfriend would change me if he/she could?

Am I willing to change myself to please my boy/girlfriend?

Do I care about pleasing my boy/girlfriend?

Do I feel I owe my boy/girlfriend anything, and if so, what?

Do I expect different things from my boy/girlfriend than I do from other people?

Do I think my boy/girlfriend expects too much from me?

Do I respect and look up to my boy/girlfriend?

Does my boy/girlfriend respect and look up to me?

Does he/she rely on me, and if so, is it too much or not enough?

What are the problems with this relationship that have always bothered me?

What are the problems which have only begun to bother me recently?

Has our relationship changed for the better, for the worse, or has our relationship not changed too much since we met?

In what ways has our relationship changed?

Does my boy/girlfriend do things that bother me?

Do I think those things are done on purpose?

Does my boy/girlfriend care if he/she annoys me?

Do I annoy my boy/girlfriend? If so, do I annoy my boy/girlfriend deliberately?

Do I think he/she is justified in being annoyed?

Does my boy/girlfriend help me in any general way?

What are some specific ways my boy/girlfriend has helped me?

Have I helped my boy/girlfriend?

Do I feel comfortable talking to my boy/girlfriend?

Are there subjects I deliberately avoid talking to him/her about, and if so, why?

Are we fairly open with each other?

What issues concerning sex am I happy about?

What issues concerning sex am I not happy about?

Do we hug and kiss—enough or too much?

How would I like to change the situation?

Are we as intimate as I would like to be?

Is my boy/girlfriend interested enough in my problems?

Does my boy/girlfriend pry too much or overly disturb my privacy?

Do I respect his/her privacy?

If I could tell my boy/girlfriend anything in the world, what would it be?

Have I already told him/her? If no, why not?

Could I tell him/her now?

Did it or would it change anything, and if so, for the better or the worse?

Does my boy/girlfriend listen when I talk to him/her?

Does he/she remember the important things I tell him/her?

Does he/she respond in a way that satisfies me?

Do I listen well to what my boy/girlfriend has to say?

Do I remember things he/she tells me?

Do I respond in a way that satisfies my boy/girlfriend?

Do we share many or very few of the same opinions?

Do we argue very much?

Are those arguments enjoyable or troublesome?

Do we fight fair or "hit below the belt"?

Does my boy/girlfriend or do I use physical force when we fight?

Do we always argue about the same things, and if so, what?

Do we raise our voices, more or less than we do with other people?

Has my boy/girlfriend hurt me in any great way? If so, was it deliberate or did he/she have good intentions?

If I could put myself in my boy/girlfriend's shoes, how would I describe his/her reason for hurting me?

Can I forgive my boy/girlfriend?

Has he/she tried to make it up to me?

Have I hurt my boy/girlfriend in any great way?

Did I hurt my boy/girlfriend deliberately or did I have good intentions or was it just an accident or side-effect?

Am I sorry and, if so, have I tried to make it up to my boy/girlfriend?

Does my boy/girlfriend forgive me?

Do I see my boy/girlfriend as much as I would like to or too much?

What things do I hate about my boy/girlfriend?

Have I told my boy/girlfriend?

Could I tell him/her?

Have I worked through the bad feelings?

Does my boy/girlfriend make me feel good or bad about myself?

Do I think my boy/girlfriend understands me better or worse than other people?

Does my boy/girlfriend restrict me in any way, and if so, in what ways?

Do the restrictions make sense to me?

Does my boy/girlfriend open up new possibilities for me, and if so, what?

Would I say my boy/girlfriend is good or bad to me?

Would I say my boy/girlfriend is good or bad for me?

Am I good to and good for my boy/girlfriend?

Am I dependent upon my boy/girlfriend or is my boy/girlfriend dependent upon me?

In what ways?

Do I like to be alone with my boy/girlfriend?

In what situations do I enjoy my boy/girlfriend most?

What things do we enjoy doing together most?

Do we have separate interests, involvements, and friends?

Do we have common interests, involvements, and friends?

Do I always/usually/rarely prefer to spend my time with my boy/girlfriend?

How much time would be just right?

Do we have enough fun together?

Am I jealous of my boy/girlfriend?

Is my boy/girlfriend jealous of me?

If my boy/girlfriend were no longer in my life, would I be sad or happy?

What would I miss?

What would I be glad about?

How would I compare my boy/girlfriend and our relationship to others I have had or would like to have?

Does this relationship take a lot away from other relationships or priorities, such as those with my family or friends?

What are the most important things to me about having a boy/girlfriend?

Do I derive those things from our relationship?

Some other problems my boy/girlfriend and I need to resolve are _____ .

Realistically, how do I see myself in terms of my love life one year from now and five years from now?

Is my present course taking me there?

What other issues concerning my love life do I want to explore?

| *Things I Like About My Relationship with My Boy/Girlfriend* | *Things I Don't Like About My Relationship with My Boy/Girlfriend* |

List as many things as possible.

Now that you've made two lists, examine them. First of all, which is longer? Which is longer when you consider only those items that are circled (the things that are important to you)? If the list of important things you don't like is much longer than the list of things you do like, you might then consider asking yourself whether or not you should change the status of your love life altogether. If the list of things you do like is much longer, you may want to concentrate instead on improving your current relationship(s).

In either case, it's time to work on changing whichever circled items that are within your control to change. So that's the next important question to ask yourself: Which items on the list of things I don't like are within my control to change? (It may help to examine the reasons these problems exist in the first place.)

P·L·A·N

What are three things I can do to change each item on the list? List everything now. Later go back and think about the conse-

A single woman's life is not particularly orderly. You have to take when the taking is good . . . the riotous living when it's offered, the quiet when there's nothing else. . . . You may marry or you may not. In today's world that is no longer the big question for women. . . . You, my friend, if you work at it, can be envied the rich, full life possible for the single woman today. It's a good show . . . enjoy it, from wherever you are, whether it's two in the balcony or one on the aisle—don't miss any of it.
—Helen Gurley Brown

quences and repercussions of each possible action. Think then, for example, if rectifying a problem will negatively affect any of the things on the other list, the things you do like about your relationship.

THINGS I CAN CHANGE

A.

B.

WAYS TO CHANGE THEM

A 1.

   2.

   3.

B 1.

   2.

   3.

*D*on't be so humble. You're not that great.
—Golda Meir

POSSIBLE CONSEQUENCES

A 1.

   2.

   3.

B 1.

   2.

   3.

Following is a list of general and specific positive actions you may want to consider taking. Not everything on the list of suggestions will apply to you nor will they all be right for you. It is hoped, though, that the list will inspire you to come up with your own ideas about how to help yourself, plan for the future, and improve your life. Not forgetting to weigh the risks and consequences, could you see yourself taking any of these actions?

TO MEET PEOPLE

I could put an ad in a personal column.

I could look through the personal columns.

I could try a dating service.

I could try to get invited to more parties.

I could have a party.

I could try to make more friends.

I could try harder to meet new people.

I could stop trying so hard to meet new people.

I could develop some new hobbies.

I could go out more with my friends.

I could ask my friends to introduce me to their other friends.

I could go out more by myself.

I could cultivate new interests.

I could buy an interesting-looking magazine that might list events I could attend.

I could try something new.

I could join a club.

I could work on being less shy.

I could let someone know that I like them.

I could take a course on a subject that interests me.

I could take up a sport.

I could take a trip with a group.

I could take a trip by myself.

I could do something I've always wanted to do.

I could ask someone for a date.

TO IMPROVE OR CHANGE A CURRENT RELATIONSHIP

I could write my boy/girlfriend a letter.

I could tell my boy/girlfriend what I've always wanted to say.

I could ask my boy/girlfriend to be honest with me.

I could try to listen better to what he/she tells me.

I could ask for his/her side of the story.

I could spend more or less time with him/her.

I could try to improve the quality of our time together.

I could confide in my boy/girlfriend more/less.

I could suggest we do something special together.

I could suggest we stop doing something that causes us trouble.

I could refuse to do something that causes us trouble.

I could try to change the way I do something.

I could try to change the way we do something.

I could try to be more independent.

I could be more/less demanding.

I could encourage my boy/girlfriend to be more/less dependent upon me.

I could help my boy/girlfriend with a problem.

I could do more to help my boy/girlfriend in general.

I could ask my boy/girlfriend to help me.

I could inform my boy/girlfriend of my problem.

I could let bygones be bygones.

I could forgive my boy/girlfriend.

I could forgive myself.

I could try to get help for dealing with my jealousy or anger.

I could try to meet new people.

I could insist we share expenses in a fairer way.

I could stop flirting with other people.

I could insist my boy/girlfriend stop flirting with other people.

I could suggest we do something romantic.

I could improve the quality of our relationship by _____ .

I could ask my boy/girlfriend to _____ .

I could ask my boy/girlfriend to stop _____ .

I could hug my boy/girlfriend.

I could tell my boy/girlfriend that I love him/her.

I could do something I know my boy/girlfriend will like.

I could ask him/her to do something for me.

I could try to become interested in my boy/girlfriend's hobbies.

We could try to develop a new mutual hobby.

I could suggest we break up.

I could suggest we see other people.

I could try to accept the fact that my boy/girlfriend is and probably will be always _____ .

I could stop _____ .

I could stop _____ .

I could stop _____ .

I could stop _____ .

I could start _____ .

I could start _____ .

I could start _____ .

I could start _____ .

I could _____ .

I could _____ .

I could _____ .

I could _____ .

I could _____ .

We could _____ .

We could _____ .

We could _____ .

We could _____ .

We could _____ .

Now it's time to . . .

A·C·T

Look at your new list and ask yourself the following questions:

Which of these things could I do or start doing today?

Which of these things take time?

Are there any first steps I can take today to achieve any of my long-term goals? (For example, if you've decided to let someone know you like them, today you could give them a sincere compliment.)

What are the things I will try to do in general?

Tell yourself, I will do at least one new thing per day until I am satisfied with the state of my relationship(s). I will do everything in my power to work within my limitations. I will try to set realistic goals and will note each accomplishment. I will perceive myself as successful just for trying, and I will be gentle with myself if things do not turn out the way I expect. If I do not accomplish something I have set out to do, I will consider the possibility that I have tried to change something that is not within my power to change, and I will try to learn lessons that will help me in this and other areas of my life. I will not expect to change everything all at once but will take things one step at a time.

The way you overcome shyness is to become so wrapped up in something that you forget to be afraid.
—Lady Bird Johnson

Things I Could Do Today:	*Things That Take Time:*

I Will Do the Following Things Today:

4. Friends

F·O·C·U·S

You may use this section to examine your friendships in general, or to look at one specific friendship. Think of one friend at a time.

Describe your friend as if he or she were a character in a novel:

Now in general terms, describe your friendship:

Make two lists side by side. On the left, list all of those things about your friendship(s) that you are happy or satisfied with. On the right, list all of the things about your friendship(s) that trouble you or that you would like to improve. You may use these questions to examine a friendship that is over; just think about the questions in the past tense. Think of everything, general and specific, important and trivial, but circle everything that is very important to you, because these are the things that will deserve special attention later.

Ask yourself any of the following questions that apply to you. If you like, jot down your answers right on the page. Then, later, transfer each answer to whichever list it fits; it's possible that some things will go on both lists:

EXAMINING YOURSELF IN RELATIONSHIP TO FRIENDS

Do I prefer to be alone or with others?

Do I prefer to be with one other person or in groups?

If extroverted, do I have enough interests and involvements to keep me happy?

If introverted, do I have enough quiet time and close friends to satisfy me?

Am I happy with the number of friends I have?

Am I happy, in general, with my friends?

Would I like to have more/fewer friends?

Do I have trouble meeting people? If so, what may be the reasons?

Do I have trouble getting close to people? If so, what may be the reasons?

Do I want to be more intimate with my friends?

Do I tend to be jealous of or about my friends?

What do I expect from my friendships?

Do I get that?

Do I have fun with my friends?

Do I fight or argue a lot with my friends?

Are these fights or arguments enjoyable or stressful?

Do I want to change my friends in specific and general ways?

Do I want to change who my friends are?

Am I comfortable making new friends?

Do I put myself in situations that make it difficult or easy to meet new people?

Do I tend to have a lot of old friends or do I constantly make new friends?

Do I have any old friends?

Which friendships do I derive more pleasure from?

Do I require that my friends meet certain qualifications?

Are there people I refuse to be friends with?

What kinds of friends do I tend to choose?

Do my different friends satisfy my different needs?

Is there anything in general about having friends that I don't like?

What do I like best about having friends?

What elements do I think go into a good friendship?

Are there any people I just don't want in my life anymore?

Why are they still here?

EXAMINING DIFFERENT FRIENDSHIPS

Examine only one friendship at a time.

Is this an old friend or a new friend?

Has this person become an old friend fast?

When I think about my friend, what are the major feelings that come to mind?

Are those feelings recent or have I felt them for a long time?

If recent, what precipitated the recent feelings?

What are the qualities of this friendship that are like my other friendships?

What are the qualities of this friendship that are different than my other friendships?

Is this my best or one of my best friends?

If I like my other friends better, why?

Do I hope to have this friendship forever?

Do I think I will?

Why do I think we became friends initially?

Are these things still true today?

How has our friendship developed over time?

Are we tolerant of each other's needs?

Would I like to be more like my friend and, if so, in what ways?

Do I think my friend would like to be more like me and, if so, in what ways?

In what ways has my friend influenced my life?

Overall, has my friend been a positive or negative influence?

Do I love my friend? Why or why not?

What are the qualities I like best in my friend?

What do I like best about our friendship?

What are the qualities I like least about my friend?

What do I like least about our friendship?

Do I expect anything from my friend that he/she gives me?

Do I expect anything from my friend that he/she denies me?

Did I used to get those things?

Would I say our friendship is equal or one-sided?

Who puts more into our friendship, me or my friend?

Do I want to put more into the friendship?

Do I wish he/she would put more into the friendship?

Do we share good things with each other?

Does one of us have more control in making decisions than the other?

Are we both happy with these arrangements?

Do we get along with each other's family and friends?

Is this a source of conflict?

Is jealousy an issue in our friendship?

How important do I think I am to my friend?

How would I change my friend if I could?

How would I change our friendship if I could?

How do I think my friend would change me if he/she could?

Am I willing to change myself to please my friend?

Do I care about pleasing my friend?

Do I feel I owe my friend anything, and if so, what?

Do I expect different things from my friend than I do from other people?

Do I think my friend expects too much from me?

Do I respect and look up to my friend?

Does my friend respect and look up to me?

Does he/she rely on me, and if so, is it too much or not enough?

What are the problems with this friendship that have always bothered me?

What are the problems which have only begun to bother me recently?

Has our friendship changed for the better, for the worse, or has our friendship not changed too much since we met?

Does my friend do things that bother me?

Do I think those things are done on purpose?

Does my friend care if he/she annoys me?

Do I annoy my friend? If so, do I annoy my friend deliberately?

Do I think he/she is justified in being annoyed?

Does my friend help me in any general way?

What are some specific ways my friend has helped me?

Have I helped my friend?

Do I feel comfortable talking to my friend?

Are there subjects I deliberately avoid talking to him/her about, and if so, why?

Are we fairly open with each other?

Are we as close as I would like to be?

When was the last time I hugged my friend, or is that something we don't do?

Do I wish we hugged more/less?

Is my friend interested enough in my problems?

Does my friend pry too much or overly disturb my privacy?

Do I respect his/her privacy?

If I could tell my friend anything in the world, what would it be?

Have I already told him/her? If no, why not?

Could I tell him/her now?

Did it or would it change anything, and if so, for the better or the worse?

Does my friend listen when I talk to him/her?

Does he/she remember the important things I tell him/her?

Does he/she respond in a way that satisfies me?

Do I listen well to what my friend has to say?

Do I remember things he/she tells me?

Do I respond in a way that satisfies my friend?

Do we share many or very few of the same opinions?

Do we argue very much?

Are those arguments enjoyable or troublesome?

Do we fight fair or "hit below the belt"?

Does my friend or do I use physical force when we fight?

Do we always argue about the same things, and if so, what?

Do we raise our voices, more or less than we do with other people?

Has my friend hurt me in any great way? If so, was it deliberate or did he/she have good intentions?

If I could put myself in my friend's shoes, how would I describe his/her reason for hurting me?

Can I forgive my friend?

Has he/she tried to make it up to me?

Have I hurt my friend in any great way?

Did I hurt my friend deliberately or did I have good intentions or was it just an accident or side-effect?

Am I sorry and, if so, have I tried to make it up to my friend?

Does my friend forgive me?

Do I forgive myself?

Do I see my friend as much as I would like to or too much?

What things do I hate about my friend?

Have I told my friend?

Could I tell him/her?

Have I worked through the bad feelings?

Does my friend make me feel good or bad about myself?

Do I do the same for my friend?

Do I think my friend understands me better or worse than other people?

Does my friend restrict me in any way, and if so, in what ways?

Do the restrictions make sense to me?

Does my friend open up new possibilities for me, and if so, what?

Would I say my friend is good or bad to me?

Am I good to and good for my friend?

Am I dependent upon my friend and/or is my friend dependent upon me?

In what ways?

Do I like to be alone with my friend?

In what situations do I enjoy my friend most?

What things do we enjoy doing together most?

Do we have separate interests, involvements, and friends?

Do we have common interests, involvements, and friends?

Do I always/usually/rarely prefer to spend my time with my friend?

Does my friendship allow me enough time to be alone?

Does my friendship allow me enough time to pursue other interests and friendships?

Do we have enough fun together?

If my friend were no longer in my life, would I be sad or happy?

What would I miss?

What would I be glad about?

How would I compare my friend and our friendship to others I have had or would like to have?

Does this friendship take a lot away from other friendships or priorities, such as those with my family or other friends?

What are the most important things to me about having a friend?

Do I derive those things from our friendship?

Some other problems my friend and I need to resolve are _____ .

Realistically, how do I see myself in terms of my friendship one year from now and five years from now?

Is my present course taking me there?

What other issues concerning my friendship do I want to explore?

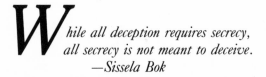

While all deception requires secrecy, all secrecy is not meant to deceive.
—Sissela Bok

Things I Like About My Friendship(s)	*Things I Don't Like About My Friendship(s)*

List as many things as possible.

A lonely person cannot, then, wait for friends to assemble around and take care of him. Friendship, for each of us, begins with reaching out. . . . When a person asks that age-old question, "What can I do about my terrible loneliness?" the best answer is still, "Do something for somebody else."
—Ann Landers, crediting Dr. Eugene Kennedy

Now that you've made two lists, examine them. First of all, which is longer? Which is longer when you consider only those items that are circled (the things that are important to you)? If the list of important things you don't like is much longer than the list of things you do like, you might then consider asking yourself whether or not you should change the status of certain friendships altogether. If the list of things you do like is much longer, you may want to concentrate instead on improving your current friendship(s).

In either case, it's time to work on changing whichever circled items that are within your control to change. So that's the next important question to ask yourself: Which items on the list of things I don't like are within my control to change? (It may help to examine the reasons these problems exist in the first place.)

P·L·A·N

What are three things I can do to change each item on the list? List everything now. Later go back and think about the consequences and repercussions of each possible action. Think then, for example, if rectifying a problem will negatively affect any of the things on the other list, the things you do like about your friendship(s).

THINGS I CAN CHANGE

A.

B.

WAYS TO CHANGE THEM

A 1.

  2.

  3.

B 1.

  2.

  3.

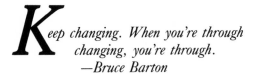

*K**eep changing. When you're through
changing, you're through.*
—*Bruce Barton*

POSSIBLE CONSEQUENCES

A 1.

   2.

   3.

B 1.

   2.

   3.

Following is a list of general and specific positive actions you may want to consider taking. Not everything on the list of suggestions will apply to you nor will they all be right for you. It is hoped, though, that the list will inspire you to come up with your own ideas about how to help yourself, plan for the future, and improve your life. Not forgetting to weigh the risks and consequences, could you see yourself taking any of these actions?

I could enroll in a class.

I could try harder to meet new people.

I could stop trying so hard to meet new people.

I could develop some new hobbies.

I could go out more with my friends.

I could go out more by myself.

I could cultivate new interests.

I could join a club.

I could work on being less shy.

I could get back in touch with someone with whom I've lost touch.

I could let someone know that I like him/her.

I could invite someone to my home.

I could write my friend a letter.

I could tell my friend what I've always wanted to say.

I could ask my friend to be honest with me.

I could try to listen better to what he/she tells me.

I could ask for his/her side of the story.

I could spend more or less time with him/her.

I could try to improve the quality of our time together.

I could confide in my friend more/less.

I could suggest we do something fun together.

I could suggest we stop doing something that causes us trouble.

I could refuse to do something that causes us trouble.

I could try to change the way I do something.

I could try to change the way we do something.

I could try to be more independent.

I could be more/less demanding.

I could encourage my friend to be more/less dependent upon me.

I could help my friend with a problem.

I could do more to help my friend in general.

I could ask my friend to help me.

I could inform my friend of my problem.

I could let bygones be bygones.

I could forgive my friend.

I could forgive myself.

I could try to deal with my jealousy or anger in ways that are positive.

I could introduce different friends to each other.

I could keep my friends more separate.

I could improve the quality of our friendship by _____ .

I could ask my friend to _____ .

I could ask my friend to stop _____ .

I could hug my friend.

I could tell my friend that I love him/her.

I could do something I know my friend will like.

I could ask him/her to do something for me.

I could try to become interested in my friend's hobbies.

We could try to develop a new mutual hobby.

I could make an effort to end the friendship.

I could try to accept the fact that my friend is and probably will be always _____ .

I could stop _____ .

I could stop _____ .

I could stop _____ .

I could stop _____ .

I could start _____ .

I could start _____ .

I could start _____ .

I could start _____ .

I could _____ .

I could _____ .

I could _____ .

I could _____ .

I could _____ .

We could _____ .

We could _____ .

We could _____ .

We could _____ .

We could _____ .

People change and forget to tell each other.
—Lillian Hellman

Now it's time to . . .

A·C·T

Look at your new list and ask yourself the following questions:

Which of these things could I do or start doing today?

Which of these things take time?

Are there any first steps I can take today to achieve any of my long-term goals? (For example, if you've decided to preserve your old friendship(s) because they are important to you, today you could call or write to someone you haven't seen in a long time.)

What are the things I will try to do in general?

Tell yourself, I will do at least one new thing per day until I am satisfied with the state of my friendship(s). I will do everything in my power to work within my limitations. I will try to set realistic goals and will note each accomplishment. I will perceive myself as successful just for trying, and I will be gentle with myself if things do not turn out the way I expect. If I do not accomplish something I have set out to do, I will consider the possibility that I have tried to change something that is not within my power to change, and I will try to learn lessons that will help me in this and other areas of my life. I will not expect to change everything all at once but will take things one step at a time.

Things I Could Do Today:	Things That Take Time:

I Will Do the Following Things Today:

5. People I Must Deal With, Like It or Not

F·O·C·U·S

This is a good place to deal with your feelings about and behavior toward coworkers, people you dislike, people who work for you, people for whom you work, neighbors, local store owners, and so on. Think of one person at a time.

Describe the person as if he or she were a character in a novel:

Now in general terms, describe your relationship with the person:

Make two lists side by side. On the left, list all of those things about your relationship that you are happy or satisfied with. On the right, list all of the things about your relationship that trouble you or that you would like to improve. Think of everything, general and specific, important and trivial, but circle everything that is very important to you, because these are the things that will deserve special attention later.

Ask yourself any of the following questions that apply to you. If you like, jot down your answers right on the page. Then, later, transfer each answer to whichever list it fits; it's possible that some things will go on both lists:

When I think about this person, what are the major feelings that come to mind?

Are those feelings recent or have I felt them for a long time?

If recent, what precipitated the recent feelings?

Do I deal with this person out of choice or is the relationship imposed upon me?

If I wanted to, could I sever this relationship?

Do I want to?

Do I have the power to change this relationship?

What is fine about this relationship?

What would I like to improve?

Could I be dealing with this person more effectively?

What do I like best about this person?

What do I like least?

What qualities do I like best about our relationship?

What qualities do I like least about our relationship?

Am I pleased with the way I respond to this person?

Does this person treat me as well as could be expected?

Does this person treat me as well as I would like?

Do I expect anything from this person that he/she gives me?

Do I expect anything from this person that he/she denies me?

Do I deal fairly with him/her?

Am I aware of any ways this person would like me to change? If so, are those changes possible or acceptable to me?

Would I like to be closer to this person?

Do I have trouble telling him/her what I feel?

If I could tell this person how I feel about him/her, what would I say?

Are there reasons I wouldn't or shouldn't say these things?

Are my feelings about this person generally negative or positive?

Under what circumstances do I like this person best?

Do I behave in a way toward this person that is detrimental to our relationship? If so, do I care?

What do I expect from our relationship?

Do I get that?

Do I have any control over how this person deals with me?

Are there reasons I have to behave in a false way with this person?

What are the qualities of this relationship that are like my other relationships?

What are the qualities of this relationship that are different than my other relationships?

Do I anticipate an end to this relationship? If so, how do I expect to feel when the relationship ends?

Why did this relationship begin?

Has the relationship changed? If so, what may be some reasons?

Are we tolerant of each other?

Would I like to be more like this person and, if so, in what ways?

Do I think this person would like to be more like me and, if so, in what ways?

In what ways has this person influenced my life?

Would I say our relationship is equal or one-sided?

Who puts more into our relationship, me or the other person?

Do I want to put more into the relationship?

Do I wish he/she would put more into the relationship?

Do we share good things with each other?

Does one of us have more control in making decisions than the other?

Are we both happy with these arrangements?

What are our sources of conflict?

Can these things be eliminated?

How important do I think I am to this person?

How would I change this person if I could?

How would I change our relationship if I could?

How do I think this person would change me if he/she could?

Am I willing to change myself to please this person?

Do I care about pleasing this person?

Are there people involved in this relationship whom I would like to please?

Do I expect different things from this person than I do from other people?

Do I think this person expects too much from me?

Do I respect this person?

Does this person respect me?

Does he/she rely on me, and if so, is it too much or not enough?

What problems have we always had with each other?

What are the problems with our relationship which have only begun to bother me recently?

Has our relationship changed for the better, for the worse, or has our relationship not changed too much since we met?

Does this person do things that bother me?

Do I think those things are done on purpose?

Does this person seem to care if he/she annoys me?

Do I annoy this person? If so, do I annoy this person deliberately?

Do I think he/she is justified in being annoyed?

Does this person help me in any general way?

What are some specific ways this person has helped me?

Have I helped this person?

Does this person listen when I talk to him/her?

Does he/she remember the important things I tell him/her?

Does he/she respond in a way that satisfies me?

Do I listen well to what this person has to say?

Do I remember things he/she tells me?

Do I respond in a way that satisfies him/her?

Do we mostly agree or disagree about things?

Do we argue very much?

Do we always argue about the same things, and if so, what?

Are these fights or arguments enjoyable or stressful?

Do we raise our voices, more or less than we do with other people?

Has this person hurt me in any great way? If so, was it deliberate or did he/she have good intentions?

If I could put myself in this person's shoes, how would I describe his/her reason for hurting me?

Can I forgive this person?

Has he/she tried to make it up to me?

Have I hurt this person in any great way? If so, did I hurt this person deliberately or did I have good intentions or was it just an accident or side-effect?

Am I sorry and, if so, have I tried to make it up to this person?

Does this person forgive me?

Do I forgive myself?

Do I see this person as much as I would like to or too much?

Does this person make me feel good or bad about myself?

Do I do the same for this person?

Do I think this person understands me better or worse than other people?

Does this person restrict me in any way, and if so, in what ways?

Do the restrictions make sense to me?

Does this person open up new possibilities for me, and if so, what?

Would I say this person is good or bad to me?

Would I say this person is good or bad for me?

Am I good to and good for this person?

Am I dependent upon this person and/or is my friend dependent upon me?

In what ways?

Do I like to be alone with this person?

In what situations do I enjoy this person most?

If this person were no longer in my life, would I be sad or happy?

What would I miss?

What would I be glad about?

A tough lesson in life that one has to learn is that not everybody wishes you well.
—Dan Rather

How would I compare this person and our relationship to others I have had or would like to have?

Some other problems this person and I need to resolve are _____ .

Realistically, how do I see myself in terms of this relationship one year from now and five years from now?

Is my present course taking me there?

What other issues concerning this relationship do I want to explore?

I'd like to reverse a traditional piece of commencement-time advice. You know it well, it goes: "Make no little plans." Instead, I'd like to say this: Make no little enemies—people with whom you differ for some petty, insignificant, personal reason. Instead, I would urge you to cultivate "mighty opposites"—people with whom you disagree on big issues, with whom you will fight to the end over fundamental convictions. And that fight, I can assure you, will be good for you and your opponent.
—Thomas J. Watson, Jr.

Things I Like About My Relationship	*Things I Don't Like About My Relationship*

List as many things as possible.

Now that you've made two lists, examine them. First of all, which is longer? Which is longer when you consider only those items that are circled (the things that are important to you)? If the list of important things you don't like is much longer than the list of things you do like, you might then consider asking yourself whether or not you should change the status of the relationship altogether. If the list of things you do like is much longer, you may want to concentrate instead on improving your current relationship.

In either case, it's time to work on changing whichever circled items that are within your control to change. So that's the next important question to ask yourself: Which items on the list of things I don't like are within my control to change? (It may help to examine the reasons these problems exist in the first place.)

P·L·A·N

What are three things I can do to change each item on the list? List everything now. Later go back and think about the consequences and repercussions of each possible action. Think then, for example, if rectifying a problem will negatively affect any of the things on the other list, the things you do like about your relationship(s).

THINGS I CAN CHANGE

A.

B.

WAYS TO CHANGE THEM

A   1.

    2.

    3.

B   1.

    2.

    3.

POSSIBLE CONSEQUENCES

A   1.

    2.

    3.

B   1.

    2.

    3.

Following is a list of general and specific positive actions you may want to consider taking. Not everything on the list of suggestions will apply to you nor will they all be right for you. It is hoped, though, that the list will inspire you to come up with

your own ideas about how to help yourself, plan for the future, and improve your life. Not forgetting to weigh the risks and consequences, could you see yourself taking any of these actions?

I could find better ways of dealing with the person.

I could be more assertive.

I could speak my mind more often.

I could try to communicate my feelings more clearly.

I could work on being less shy.

I could let the person know that I like him/her.

I could smile at him/her more often.

I could invite the person to my home.

I could compliment him/her more often.

I could let the person know what I don't like about him/her.

I could be nicer to the person.

I could stop being friendly toward the person.

I could encourage the person to behave differently toward me.

I could write the person a letter.

I could avoid the person.

I could tell the person what I've always wanted to say.

I could ask the person to be honest with me.

I could try a new tactic for dealing with the person.

I could try to listen better to what he/she tells me.

I could ask for his/her side of the story.

I could spend more or less time with him/her.

I could try to improve the quality of our time together.

I could confide in the person more/less.

I could suggest we do something fun together.

I could suggest we stop doing something that causes us trouble.

I could refuse to do something that causes us trouble.

I could try to change the way I do something.

I could try to change the way we do something.

I could try to be more independent.

I could be more/less demanding.

I could encourage the person to be more/less dependent upon me.

I could help the person with a problem.

I could do more to help the person in general.

I could ask the person to help me.

I could inform the person of my problem.

I could let bygones be bygones.

I could forgive the person.

I could forgive myself.

I could try to deal with my jealousy or anger in ways that are positive.

I could try to stay calm when we fight.

I could think of ways to avoid fighting or arguing.

I could try to replace this person in my life.

I could improve the quality of our relationship by _____ .

I could ask this person to _____ .

I could ask this person to stop _____ .

I could hug this person.

I could do something I know this person will like.

I could ask him/her to do something for me.

I could make an effort to end the relationship.

I could try to accept the fact that this person is and probably will always be _____ .

I could stop _____ .

I could stop _____ .

I could stop _____ .

I could stop _____ .

I could start _____ .

I could start _____ .

I could start _____ .

I could start _____ .

I could _____ .

I could _____ .

I could _____ .

We could _____ .

We could _____ .

We could _____ .

We could _____ .

We could _____ .

Now it's time to . . .

A·C·T

Look at your new list and ask yourself the following questions:

Which of these things could I do or start doing today?

Which of these things take time?

Are there any first steps I can take today to achieve any of my long-term goals? (For example, if you've decided to find a new employee, today you could ask around for recommendations.)

What are the things I will try to do in general?

Tell yourself, I will do at least one new thing per day until I am satisfied with the state of my relationship(s). I will do everything in my power to become satisfied with my limitations. I will try to set realistic goals, and I will concentrate more on being happy about my accomplishments. I will perceive myself as successful just for trying, and I will be gentle with myself if things do not turn out the way I expect. If I do not accomplish something I have set out to do, I will consider the possibility that I have tried to change something that is not altogether within my power to change, and I will try to learn lessons that will help me in this and other areas of my life. I will not try to do everything all at once but will take things one step at a time.

Things I Could Do Today:	*Things That Take Time:*

I Will Do the Following Things Today:

E·V·A·L·U·A·T·E

I will keep a list here of all of the things I've done and the results I've achieved:

DATE   STEP TAKEN   RESULTS

III.

MY HOME AND COMMUNITY

1. Living Environment
2. Neighborhood
3. Hobbies and Leisure Activities

1. Living Environment

F·O·C·U·S

This is how someone who's never been here might describe my living environment (the people I live with and the interior of my home—the neighborhood is dealt with in the next section):

This is how I would describe my living environment:

Make two lists side by side. On the left, list all of those things about your living environment that you feel good about and are satisfied with. On the right, list all of the things about your home that trouble you. Think of everything, general and specific, important and trivial, but circle everything that is very important to you, because these are the things that will deserve special attention later.

Be sure to ask yourself any of the following questions that apply to you. If you like, jot down your answers right on the page. Then, later, transfer each answer to whichever list it fits; it's possible that some things will go on both lists:

What are the main problems about my home that always bother me?

What do I like best about living here?

What is the most important thing about "home" to me?

Do I use all of the rooms of my home?

Specifically and generally, how do I feel about each room?

Where do I spend most of my time?

Is there anything I keep tripping over?

Does anything make me feel bad when I look at it?

Which pieces of furniture and furnishings do I like the best and least?

Is my home decorated and furnished in the way that appeals to me the most?

Would certain rooms look better if I moved around the furniture?

Do other people always complain about something in my home that I like a lot?

Does it matter to me?

Do they live here, too?

Do I like the colors of my walls and the look of my floor?

What things are in need of repair?

Would I like to replace anything and with what?

Can I afford to make the changes I envision?

154 Do I like clutter or a simple, minimalist look?

*I*f fifty million people say a foolish thing, it is
still a foolish thing.
—Anatole France

Do I keep anything just for nostalgia?

Do I want my home to reflect me and does it?

Does my home suit my personality?

Do I need a change?

Do I hold on to things too long?

Do I throw things away and then have regrets?

Do I enjoy getting rid of things?

Are there many things that I never look at or use?

How would I feel if I got rid of those things?

Should I consider selling things or giving them to charity?

Am I handy enough to make changes instead of hiring outsiders or buying new things?

Do I know someone who could save me money on proposed changes?

Are there any large purchases I want to save up for?

Whom do I live with?

Do they feel basically the same way about where we live?

Is it important to me how they feel about where we live?

Do I control the environment more or do they?

*F*ind out where the people want to go, then hustle
    yourself around in front of them.
                    —*James Kilpatrick*

Did I or someone else put together my living environment?

Who does the environment mean the most to?

Who spends the most time here?

How do we differ in our living needs?

Is there any way we can both or all have our way?

What compromises can we make to live harmoniously?

Do I have a space that is all my own, that everyone respects?

Is the same true for everyone who lives here?

Does everyone who lives here have enough privacy?

Is there enough community space here, where people can interact well?

Am I basically happy or unhappy with the people I live with?

Do I have or want pets?

Do I have or want children?

Are they or would they be comfortable in this environment?

What changes should I or do I want to make to accommodate them?

Do people like to visit me?

Do I like when people visit me?

Is it important to me if my home is neat and clean and do I keep it that way?

Do I feel the housework is shared fairly or to everyone's satisfaction?

Are there other people's homes I like better than mine? If so, what things do I like better about their homes?

Do I want to make my home more like theirs?

Do I feel safe at home?

What bothers me the most about my environment?

Is this home temporary, long-term, or permanent?

If I moved or made changes, what would I like to remain the same about my living situation?

Realistically, how do I see myself in terms of my home one year from now and five years from now?

Is my present course taking me there?

What other issues regarding my home do I want to explore?

The danger of the past was that men became slaves. The danger of the future is that men may become robots.
—Erich Fromm

Things I Like About My Home	Things I Don't Like About My Home
List as many things as possible.	

Now that you've made two lists, it's time to examine them. First of all, which is longer? Which is longer when you consider only those items that are circled (the things that are important to you)?

If the list of important things you don't like is much longer than the list of things you do like, you might then consider asking yourself whether or not you should change your living environment altogether. In either case, it's time to work on changing whichever circled items that are within your control to change.

So that's the next important question to ask yourself: Which items on the list of things I don't like are within my control to change? (It may help to examine the reasons these problems exist in the first place.)

P·L·A·N

What are three things I can do to change each item on the list? List everything now. Later go back and think about the consequences and repercussions of each possible action. Think then, for example, if rectifying a problem will negatively affect any of the things on the other list, the things you do like about your home.

THINGS I CAN CHANGE

A.

B.

WAYS TO CHANGE THEM

A   1.

     2.

     3.

B   1.

     2.

     3.

POSSIBLE CONSEQUENCES

A   1.

     2.

     3.

B   1.

     2.

     3.

Following is a list of general and specific positive actions you may want to consider taking. Not everything on the list of suggestions will apply to you nor will they all be right for you. It is hoped, though, that the list will inspire you to come up with your own ideas about how to help yourself, plan for the future,

and improve your life. Not forgetting to weigh the risks and consequences, could you see yourself taking any of these actions?

I could rearrange my furniture.

I could refurnish and redecorate by myself or with an expert or friend.

I could read a "home environment" magazine.

I could have the _____ repaired.

I could buy or save for something new.

I could give away, throw out, or sell _____.

I could go through my closets.

I could clean more thoroughly.

I could make my bed every morning.

I could hire a cleaning person.

I could renovate one room or do a major renovation.

I could add another room.

I could change the use of one of the rooms or areas.

I could find another place to store my _____.

I could reorganize the _____.

I could paint or wallpaper my walls.

I could buy a new rug or carpet.

I could have the floors sanded and polished or tiled.

I could get new hardware for the drawers.

I could refinish the furniture.

I could organize my files.

I could soundproof the room.

I could get an alarm system.

I could arrange to live with someone else.

I could invite someone to visit or have a party.

I could spend more time at home or get out more.

I could get a pet or give away a pet.

I could be more careful when I _____.

I could set aside more or less time for _____.

I could complain to _____ about _____.

I could move.

I will try to accept the fact that my home is _____.

I will try to accept the fact that I live with _____.

I could stop _____.

I could stop _____.

I could start _____.

I could start _____.

I could _____.

I could _____.

I could _____.

I could _____.

Now it's time to . . .

A·C·T

Look at your new list and ask yourself the following questions:

Which of these things could I do or start doing today?

Which of these things take time?

Are there any first steps I can take today to achieve any of my long-term goals? (For example, if you've decided to renovate your bathroom, today you could start getting estimates on what it would cost and make a list of what you'd like in your new bathroom.)

What are the general things I will try to do?

Tell yourself, I will do at least one new thing per day until I am satisfied with my living environment. I will do everything in my power to work within my limitations. I will try to set realistic goals and will note each accomplishment. I will perceive myself as successful just for trying, and I will be gentle with myself if things do not turn out the way I expect. If I do not accomplish

*D*ecision is a risk rooted in the courage of being free.
—Paul Tillich

something I have set out to do, I will consider the possibility that I have tried to change something that is not within my power to change, and I will try to learn lessons that will help me in this and other areas of my life. I will not expect to change everything all at once but will take things one step at a time.

Things I Could Do Today:	*Things That Take Time:*

I Will Do the Following Things Today:

2. Neighborhood

F·O·C·U·S

How would I describe my neighborhood to someone who was thinking about moving here? How do I feel about my neighborhood?

Make two lists side by side. On the left, list all of those things about your neighborhood that you feel good about and are satisfied with. On the right, list all of the things about your neighborhood that trouble you. Think of everything, general and specific, important and trivial, but circle everything that is very important to you, because these are the things that will deserve special attention later.

Ask yourself any of the following questions that apply to you. If you like, jot down your answers right on the page. Then, later, transfer each answer to whichever list it fits; it's possible that some things will go on both lists:

What are the main problems about my neighborhood that always bother me?

Where would I live if I could live anywhere in the world?

Why don't I live there?

Compared to my ideal place, what is the same about living where I am?

What is different about living where I am?

What is worse about living where I am?

What is better about living where I am?

What are the best features of this neighborhood?

What are the worst features of this neighborhood?

Do I prefer the country or the city or the suburbs?

What are the most important features of a neighborhood to me?

Do I prefer to live in a house, condo, coop, rental apartment, or other?

Do I know my neighbors?

Do I care to know my neighbors?

Do I care whether or not I have neighbors?

Do I like to have friends pop in and do they?

What facilities are nearby that I use?

What facilities are nearby that I like to have nearby?

What facilities do I wish were nearby?

What or whom might be worth moving to be near?

Do I have family nearby?

Do I want to have family nearby?

*T*here is no greater challenge than to have someone
relying upon you; no greater satisfaction than to
vindicate his expectation.
—Kingman Brewster

Is my neighborhood pretty?

Do I care whether or not my neighborhood is pretty?

Do I feel like I'm part of my neighborhood?

Do I participate in neighborhood events?

Do I belong to any neighborhood clubs or organizations?

Do I participate in community politics?

Do my politics match those of my community?

Is that something that is important to me?

Do I want my neighbors to be like me? Are they?

How would I like them to be different?

How would I like to be more like them?

Do the people I live with feel like I do about the neighborhood?

What do they like and not like about it?

Do I feel at home in this neighborhood?

Do I feel safe in this neighborhood?

Do the people I live with feel safe in this neighborhood?

Is there anything very wrong about this neighborhood?

Is it easy to get to work?

Can I afford to live somewhere I would like better?

Did I ever live anywhere I preferred more? If so, what did I prefer about that place?

Do I like living in a place for a long time or do I prefer to move more frequently?

Have I lived here too long or not long enough to know?

Does living in this neighborhood make it easy or hard to do things I like or need to do (such as shopping)?

Do I wish I owned my own home?

Do I think owning a home is a burden?

Can I afford or do I think I'll ever afford to move to a better neighborhood?

Am I sorry to see that my neighborhood's changed or glad to see progress?

Do I wish my neighborhood would change and how?

Do I anticipate a need to move and why?

Do I need a change?

Of the people I live with, who does the neighborhood mean most to?

---

*H*e who cannot rest, cannot work; he who cannot let go, cannot hold on; he who cannot find footing, cannot go forward.
—*Harry Emerson Fosdick*

Do I spend a lot of time in my neighborhood?

Do the people I live with spend a lot of time here?

Would they or I be sorry to move?

How do we differ in our neighborhood needs?

Is there any way we can both or all have our way?

Do I have or want children in the near future?

Are they or would they be comfortable in this neighborhood?

Is there anything I can do to better my neighborhood?

Would it be easier to help change this neighborhood or to move to a different neighborhood?

Whether I stay or move, what would I like or need to remain the same about my neighborhood?

Can I think of people whose neighborhoods I prefer to mine?

What do I like better about their neighborhood?

What do I like better about my neighborhood?

Where would I like to be living one year from now and five years from now?

Is my present course taking me there?

What other issues regarding my neighborhood do I want to explore?

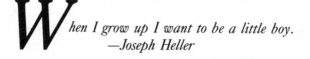

When I grow up I want to be a little boy.
—Joseph Heller

Things I Like About My Neighborhood	Things I Don't like About My Neighborhood

List as many things as possible.

I'm just a plowhand from Arkansas, but I have learned how to hold a team together. How to lift some men up, how to calm down others, until finally they've got one heartbeat, together, a team. There's just three things I ever say. If anything goes bad, then I did it. If anything goes semigood, then we did it. If anything goes real good, then you did it. That's all it takes to get people to win football games for you.
—Bear Bryant

Now that you've made two lists, examine them. Which is longer? Which is longer when you consider only those items that are circled (the things that are important to you)?

If the list of important things you don't like is much longer than the list of things you do like, you might then consider moving. In either case, it's time to work on changing whichever circled items that are within your control to change.

So that's the next important question to ask yourself: Which items on the list of things I don't like are within my control to change? (It may help to examine the reasons these problems exist in the first place.)

P·L·A·N

What are three things I can do to change each item on the list? List everything now. Later go back and think about the consequences and repercussions of each possible action, whether rectifying a problem will negatively affect any of the things on the other list, the things you do like about your neighborhood.

THINGS I CAN CHANGE

A.

B.

WAYS TO CHANGE THEM

A   1.

   2.

   3.

B   1.

   2.

   3.

POSSIBLE CONSEQUENCES

A   1.

   2.

   3.

B   1.

   2.

   3.

Following is a list of general and specific positive actions you may want to consider taking. Not everything on the list of suggestions will apply to you nor will they all be right for you. It is hoped, though, that the list will inspire you to come up with your own ideas about how to help yourself, plan for the future, and improve your life. Not forgetting to weigh the risks and consequences, could you see yourself taking any of these actions?

I could buy a house.

I could read a book about home buying.

I could paint my house.

I could start using some of the local facilities.

I could do something to beautify the neighborhood.

I could welcome my new neighbor.

I could meet my old neighbor.

I could do something nice for my neighbor.

I could build a fence between me and my neighbor.

I could visit the town hall.

I could attend a local meeting.

I could stop being involved in community politics.

I could initiate a block cleanup.

I could join in the block cleanup.

I could arrange a block party.

I could start a new club.

I could start taking the bus to work.

I could form a car pool.

I could send my child to a private school.

I could attend a PTA meeting.

I could get a local job.

I could teach a course locally.

I could finally explore the local park.

I could visit different neighborhoods.

I could read about different neighborhoods.

I could ask people about where they live or where they like living.

I could keep a list of neighborhoods I prefer to mine.

I could see a real estate broker.

I could take a course in real estate.

I could read a book about real estate.

I could look at new apartments.

I could buy a coop or condo.

I could read the real estate section of the newspaper every day.

I could circle items in it that interest me.

I could help an elderly or needy neighbor.

I could baby-sit.

I could put my home up for sale.

I could find out what other properties are selling for in my neighborhood.

I could rent or buy a place in the country.

I could rent or buy a place in the city.

I could commute.

I could find a place closer to the _____ .

I could find a place farther from the _____ .

I could come home earlier.

I could shop for a mortgage.

I could get a second mortgage.

I could save money to afford a _____ .

I will try to accept the fact that my neighborhood is _____ .

I could sacrifice _____ now for the sake of future _____ .

I could stop _____ .

I could stop _____ .

I could start _____ .

I could start _____ .

I could _____ .

I could _____ .

I could _____ .

I could _____ .

L *ong-range planning does not deal with future deci-*
sions, but with the future of present decisions.
—Peter Drucker

Now it's time to . . .

A·C·T

Look at your new list and ask yourself the following questions:

Which of these things could I do or start doing today?

Which of these things take time?

Are there any first steps I can take today to achieve any of my long-term goals? (For example, if you've decided to find out why your cousin loves living in Albuquerque, you could start making plans to visit today by calling or writing to her or by finding out the price of an airline ticket there.)

What are the general things I will try to do?

Tell yourself, I will do at least one new thing per day until I am satisfied with my neighborhood. I will do everything in my power to work within my limitations. I will try to set realistic goals and will note each accomplishment. I will perceive myself as successful just for trying, and I will be gentle with myself if things do not turn out the way I expect. If I do not accomplish something I have set out to do, I will consider the possibility that I have tried to change something that is not within my power to change, and I will try to learn lessons that will help me in this and other areas of my life. I will not expect to change everything all at once but will take things one step at a time.

Things I Could Do Today:	*Things That Take Time:*

I Will Do the Following Things Today:

3. Hobbies and Leisure Activities

F·O·C·U·S

If someone asked me what my hobbies and leisure activities were, I would tell them this:

This is how I feel about my current hobbies and leisure time:

Make two lists side by side. On the left, list all of those things about your hobbies and leisure activities that you feel good about and are satisfied with. On the right, list all of the things about your hobbies and leisure activities that trouble you. Think of everything, general and specific, important and trivial, but circle everything that is very important to you, because these are the things that will deserve special attention later.

Ask yourself any of the following questions that apply to you.

If you like, jot down your answers right on the page. Then,

later, transfer each answer to whichever list it fits; it's possible that some things will go on both lists:

What do I spend most of my leisure time doing?

Do I enjoy my hobbies and leisure activities?

What do I enjoy about them?

What do I not enjoy about them?

Do I have enough leisure time to spend doing what I enjoy doing?

Is there anything about my hobbies that I dislike?

Why do I choose to spend my leisure the way I do?

What are some other people's hobbies that appeal to me?

Why haven't I tried them?

Ideally, how would I like to spend my leisure time?

Is that how I would like to spend it? Why or why not?

Would I like to have more leisure time than I have?

Is there a way to get it?

What are the main problems associated with my hobby or hobbies?

Do my leisure activities suit my talents and temperament?

Do I like my hobbies to be fun or to give me a sense of achievement or both?

Do I like competition?

Do I think of myself as competitive?

Do I hate losing?

Am I a good sport?

Do I curse when I play—for example when I miss or when I do something incorrectly?

Do I prefer solitary hobbies or ones that involve another person or many other people?

Do I want my hobbies to expend energy, make me excited, or relax me?

Do my hobbies do that?

Am I a fast learner?

Do I like games?

Is there anything I'm particularly knowledgeable about or good at?

Would I enjoy a new hobby associated with that knowledge or skill?

Do I collect anything?

Do I like to be associated with any particular hobby or with several ones?

Do I use hobbies to meet people?

Are my leisure activities generally solo, with one other person, or in groups?

Do I like it that way?

Do I think there may be a hobby that I'd enjoy that I've never tried?

Do I have the necessary skills or would I have to acquire them?

Do I like creating things?

*T*ake an object. Do something to it.
Do something else to it.
—Jasper Johns

Are my hobbies goal oriented?

Have I given up any old hobbies? If so, do I miss them?

Is there a good reason why I don't do them anymore?

Are there any hobbies I've never tried that sound appealing to me?

Do I have a project that I've always wanted to get around to that I've never gotten around to?

Is it possible that I don't really want to do it?

Do I work hard at my play or does it come easy to me?

Do I have lots of hobbies, none, or very few?

Are hobbies important to me or a waste of time?

Are there any risks associated with my current leisure activities?

Are there any risks associated with the leisure activities I contemplate doing?

Are the activities worth the risks?

Do I like risks?

What obstacles are keeping me from doing the leisure activities that I would enjoy most?

Do I take my hobbies seriously?

183

*Y*ou must learn day by day, year by year, to broaden
your horizon. The more things you love, the more
you are interested in, the more you enjoy, the more you are
indignant about—the more you have left when anything happens.
—Ethel Barrymore

Do I combine my hobbies with my chores?

What are the interests or issues that really engage me?

Have I spent much time taking part in those interests and
issues lately?

Do I know what resources are available in my community and
am I making use of them?

Am I or would I like to be a joiner?

Do I belong to any clubs or organizations?

Would I or do I enjoy doing any volunteer work or other community activity? If so, what do I get out of my involvement in
them?

Do I have any limitations that keep me from pursuing
my interests?

Do my hobbies stimulate me intellectually?

Am I happy with the extent to which my mind is engaged?

Do I pursue cultural activities in a way that suits me?

Do I like to read, and if so, do I read as much as I would like?

Are there any books I would like to read?

What subjects would I like to know more about?

Have I taken any classes since I went to school, and were they satisfying? Am I satisfied with my social life?

Do I have enough time to see people and to do things that are important to me?

Are there pressures or problems interfering with my enjoyment of my leisure time?

Do I intend to be pursuing the same hobbies and leisure activities one year or five years from now?

Are my hobbies and leisure time activities associated with any goals that I would like to achieve over the next five years?

Is there anything I want to achieve in my spare time over the next five years?

Realistically, where would I like to be in terms of my hobbies and leisure time one and five years from now?

Is my present course taking me there?

What other issues regarding my hobbies and leisure time do I want to explore?

*F*or fast-acting relief, try slowing down.
      —*Lily Tomlin*

*T*ry as much as possible to be wholly alive, with all your might, and when you laugh, laugh like hell and when you get angry, get good and angry. Try to be alive. You will be dead soon enough.
      —*William Saroyan*

Things I Like About My Hobbies and Leisure Time	Things I Don't Like About My Hobbies and Leisure Time

List as many things as possible.

*I*t is better to have loafed and lost than never
to have loafed at all.
—James Thurber

*W*hen in charge, ponder. When in trouble,
delegate. When in doubt, mumble.
—Good Life Almanac

Now that you've made two lists, it's time to examine them. First of all, which is longer? Which is longer when you consider only those items that are circled (the things that are important to you)?

If the list of important things you don't like is much longer than the list of things you do like, you might then consider some new hobbies. If the list of things you do like is longer, you should probably concentrate instead on continuing your old hobbies. In either case, it's time to work on changing whichever circled items that are within your control to change.

So that's the next important question to ask yourself: Which items are on the list of things I don't like are within my control to change? (It may help to examine the reasons these problems exist in the first place.)

P·L·A·N

What are three things I can do to change each item on the list? List everything now. Later go back and think about the consequences and repercussions of each possible action. Think then, for example, if rectifying a problem will negatively affect any of the things on the other list, the things you do like about your current hobbies and leisure activities.

THINGS I CAN CHANGE

A.

B.

WAYS TO CHANGE THEM

A 1.

   2.

   3.

B 1.

   2.

   3.

POSSIBLE CONSEQUENCES

A 1.

   2.

   3.

B 1.

   2.

   3.

Following is a list of general and specific positive actions you may want to consider taking. Not everything on the list of suggestions will apply to you nor will they all be right for you. It is hoped, though, that the list will inspire you to come up with your own ideas about how to help yourself, plan for the future,

and improve your life. Not forgetting to weigh the risks and consequences, could you see yourself taking any of these actions?

I could subscribe to a magazine.

I could read a book on a subject I know.

I could read a book on a subject I don't know.

I could ask my friends to tell me what they like about their hobbies.

I could buy or save for a _____ .

I could try to be less or more aggressive when I play.

I could make a reservation to _____ .

I could work at being a good sport.

I could teach someone else my hobby.

I could ask someone else to teach me theirs.

I could enroll in a course.

I could give up leisure activities from which I derive no benefit or which aren't fun anymore.

I could try to find a hobby that suits my talents.

I could try to find a hobby that suits my temperament.

I could try to find a hobby that relaxes me.

I could try to find a hobby that makes me think or work harder.

I could try to leave work earlier.

I could go to the hobbies section of the library or bookstore.

I could watch less television.

I could join a club.

I could start a club.

I could do volunteer work.

I could become involved in my community.

I could take a trip.

I could travel to _____ .

I could practice.

I could spend more time at it.

I could ask someone to help me.

I could try skiing, writing, collecting, painting, drawing, sewing, renovating, playing, building, a new sport, biking, riding, hiking, walking, tennis, chess, a musical instrument, moviegoing, sailing, and so on.

I could stop _____ .

I could stop _____ .

I could start _____ .

I could start _____ .

I could _____ .

I could _____ .

*L*ife is short; live it up.
    —Nikita S. Khrushchev

Now it's time to . . .

A·C·T

Look at your new list and ask yourself the following questions:

Which of these things could I do or start doing today?

Which of these things take time?

Are there any first steps I can take today to achieve any of my long-term goals? (For example, if you've decided to take up tennis, today you could find out what courts are available to you.)

What are the general things I will try to do?

Tell yourself, I will do at least one new thing per day until I am satisfied with how I feel about my leisure time. I will do everything in my power to work within my limitations. I will try to set realistic goals and will note each accomplishment. I will perceive myself as successful just for trying, and I will be gentle with myself if things do not turn out the way I expect. If I do not accomplish something I have set out to do. I will consider the possibility that I have tried to change something that is not within my power to change, and I will try to learn lessons that

will help me in this and other areas of my life. I will not expect
to change everything all at once but will take things one step at
a time.

Things I Could Do Today:	Things That Take Time:

I Will Do the Following Things Today:

*We must learn to be still in the midst of activity
and to be vibrantly alive in repose.*
—*Indira Gandhi*

E·V·A·L·U·A·T·E

I will keep a list of all of the things I've done and the results I've achieved:

DATE	STEP TAKEN	RESULTS

IV.

MY WORK AND SCHOOL

1. Work
2. Financial Condition
3. School

1. Work

F·O·C·U·S

When I meet somebody new and they ask me, "What do you do?" this is what I tell them:

But there's more to my work than that; this is what I actually and specifically do:

Make two lists side by side. On the left, list all of those things about your work that you like. On the right, list all of the things about your work that you don't like. Think of everything, general and specific, important and trivial, but circle everything that is very important to you, because these are the things that will deserve special attention later.

Ask yourself any of the following questions that apply to you. If you like, jot down your answers right on the page. Then,

*I*f you doubt you can accomplish something, then you can't accomplish it. You have to have confidence in your ability, and then be tough enough to follow through.
—*Rosalynn Carter*

later, transfer each answer to whichever list it fits; it's possible that some things will go on both lists:

Do I work too hard, not hard enough, or about the right amount for me?

Do I prefer working for myself or for someone else?

Does it take me very long to get to and from work and do I enjoy the trip?

How are my hours?

Do I like the environment I work in?

Am I comfortable in my work place?

Do I like the people I work with or for?

Is there autonomy, and is that something I want?

Do I enjoy the routine tasks associated with my work?

Are there special assignments that I particularly enjoy?

Does my work generate feelings of reward and satisfaction or is it just a way to earn money?

Do I earn enough money to suit my needs?

Do I feel underpaid, properly paid, or overpaid?

How is my energy level at work and after work?

Does my work allow for enough leisure time?

Is my work recognized?

Does my work utilize my best talents and skills?

Does my work utilize the talents and skills that I enjoy utilizing?

Are my mind and education being properly utilized?

What are five other specific things about my work that I like and don't like?

Are there any risks associated with this work?

Do I feel secure in my work?

Am I building a successful future, monetarily and otherwise?

Is this something I want to be doing in five years?

Is this something that is leading to what I'd like to be doing in five years?

If and when I retire, would I like it to be from this?

Realistically, how do I see myself in terms of my work one year from now and five years from now?

Is my present course taking me there?

What other issues regarding my work do I want to explore?

Luck? I don't know anything about luck. I've never banked on it, and I'm afraid of people who do. Luck to me is something else: hard work—and realizing what is opportunity and what isn't.
—Lucille Ball

Things I Like About My Work	*Things I Don't Like About My Work*

List as many things as possible.

A musician must make music, an artist must paint, a poet must write, if he is to be ultimately at peace with himself. What a man can be, he must be.
—*Abraham Harold Maslow*

T he one important thing I have learned over the years is the difference between taking one's work seriously and taking one's self seriously. The first is imperative and the second is disastrous.
—*Margot Fonteyn*

Now that you've made two lists, it's time to examine them. First of all, which is longer? Which is longer when you consider only those items that are circled (the things that are important to you)?

If the list of important things you don't like is much longer than the list of things you do like, you might then consider asking yourself whether or not you should begin looking for new work. If the list of things you do like is much longer, you may want to concentrate instead on improving your current work. In either case, it's time to work on changing whichever circled items that are within your control to change.

So that's the first and most important question to ask yourself: Which items on the list of things I don't like are within my control to change? (It may help to examine the reasons these problems exist in the first place.)

P·L·A·N

What are three things I can do to change each item on the list? List everything now. Later go back and think about the consequences and repercussions of each possible action. Think then, for example, if rectifying a problem will negatively affect any of the things on the other list, the things you do like about your work.

THINGS I CAN CHANGE

A.

B.

WAYS TO CHANGE THEM

A 1.

   2.

   3.

B 1.

   2.

   3.

POSSIBLE CONSEQUENCES

A 1.

   2.

   3.

B 1.

   2.

   3.

Following is a list of general and specific positive actions you may want to consider taking. Not everything on the list of suggestions will apply to you nor will they all be right for you. It is hoped, though, that the list will inspire you to come up with your own ideas about how to help yourself, plan for the future,

and improve your life. Not forgetting to weigh the risks and consequences, could you see yourself taking any of these actions?

I could go back to school full time.

I could take an evening course.

I could redo my résumé.

I could be more aggressive.

I could make a few phone calls.

I could dress more professionally.

I could be nicer to certain associates.

I could ask for a promotion.

I could ask for more money.

I could work longer hours.

I could come home earlier.

I could buy a car and drive to work.

I could ask for _____.

I could get a different job that might lead to the job I want.

I could change careers and be a _____or
a _____.

I could use my qualifications to become a _____.

I could become qualified to be a _____.

I could talk to a job counselor.

I could practice a skill.

I could do library research.

I could save capital.

I could go through the want ads in Sunday's paper.

I could redecorate my work place.

I could take a vacation.

I could move to the country or to another city.

I could buy a computer.

I could hire someone to help me.

I could tell the boss to make his/her own coffee.

I could do a promotional mailing.

I could advertise in the local paper.

I could start _____ .

I could start _____ .

I could stop _____ .

I could stop _____ .

I could _____ .

I could _____ .

I could _____ .

I could _____ .

I could _____ .

Now it's time to . . .

A·C·T

Look at your new list and ask yourself the following questions:

Which of these things could I do or start doing today?

Which of these things take time?

Are there any first steps I can take to day to achieve any of my long-term goals? (For example, if you've decided that you may want to go back to school, today you could send away for catalogs.)

What are the general things I will try to do?

Tell yourself, I will do at least one new thing per day until I am satisfied with my work. I will do everything in my power to work within my limitations. I will try to set realistic goals and will note each accomplishment. I will perceive myself as successful just for trying, and I will be gentle with myself if things do not turn out the way I expect. If I do not accomplish something I have set out to do, I will consider the possibility that I have tried to change something that is not within my power to change, and I will try to learn lessons that will help me in this and other areas of my life. I will not expect to change everything all at once but will take things one step at a time.

Things I Could Do Today:	*Things That Take Time:*

I Will Do the Following Things Today:

*N*ever continue in a job you don't enjoy. If you're
happy in what you're doing, you'll like yourself,
you'll have inner peace. And if you have that, along with
physical health, you will have had more success than you
could possibly have imagined.
—*Johnny Carson*

2. *Financial Condition*

F·O·C·U·S

This is how I would describe my current financial situation:

This is how much money I have:

This is a list of my assets:

This is how much I think my assets are currently worth:

These are my debts (including credit cards):

This is how much I earn:

Make two lists side by side. On the left, list all of those things about your financial condition that you like or are satisfied with. On the right, list all of the things about your financial condition that you don't like or are dissatisfied with. Think of everything, general and specific, important and trivial, but circle everything that is very important to you, because these are the things that will deserve special attention later.

Ask yourself any of the following questions that apply to you. If you like, jot down your answers right on the page. Then, later, transfer each answer to whichever list it fits; it's possible that some things will go on both lists:

In five years I expect to have saved up: $————.

I have assets worth $————.

In five years I expect to be earning $————.

Am I satisfied with that projection?

Will I need to change my spending habits to achieve that?

What are my spending habits like now?

Do I know my spending priorities, and if so, what are they?

Are my spending habits more oriented toward the past, present, or future?

What do I wish I could spend less on?

What expenses can I not rid myself of?

Do I know how much I spend in interest on credit cards?

What might I spend more on?

Do I know how to save money?

Do I have clear-cut financial goals?

If I am saving money, what is it for?

Is my savings invested in a way that makes sense for my financial needs?

If I am not saving money, why not?

Do I wish I could?

How might I cut corners?

On what could I spend less?

Is there anything I should consider saving for?

Do I know anyone who is saving for something big?

Is that something I might want to save for also?

Besides cutting corners, are there other ways I might save such as investing?

Do I have investments?

Do I know everything I need to or care to know about investing?

The largest purchase I expect to make over the next five years is _____ .

Is my financial situation changing, and if so, is it improving or getting worse?

What financial changes do I expect which are outside my control?

What changes do I expect that may be within my control?

Do I have insurance?

Do I have stock?

Do I have a broker? If so, am I satisfied with the work that broker does for me? If not, do I need one?

*N*ever underestimate the value of luck, but remember
that luck comes to those searching for something.
—*Stanley Marcus*

Am I happy with my bank?

Do I have a financial advisor?

Would I benefit from having a financial advisor?

Can I afford all of the things that I want?

Do I expect to be able to afford all of the things I want over the next five years?

What am I willing to do to obtain these things?

Have I ever been on a budget?

Do I think I could benefit from being on a budget?

How strict a budget could I live with?

Do I live within my means or above my means?

Do I sacrifice too much?

Do people call me a spendthrift or a cheapskate or a wise investor?

Do I agree with them?

Would I like to change that?

Do I manage to get what I want?

What are my feelings about money?

Do I lie about money?

Do I cheat or steal and, if so, do I feel guilty?

Would I cheat or steal?

How important is money to me?

Do I place not enough importance, too much importance, or just about the right amount of importance on money?

Am I charitable?

Am I satisfied with my attitudes toward money?

Where do I think my attitudes about money originated?

Am I proud of any financial accomplishments?

Have I made any great financial mistakes? If so, am I happy with how I handled the results?

Do I seem to learn from my financial mistakes?

Am I generous?

Am I too generous?

Do I feel cheated?

When I think about it, have I really been cheated (regularly, now and then, by one person, by everybody, in general)?

Am I afraid of being cheated? Do I know why?

Has anyone stolen from me and, if so, has this affected my attitudes about money?

Am I jealous of people who have more than I?

Am I financially secure?

Am I satisfied with my financial situation?

Am I afraid of losing what I have?

I've never been poor, only broke. Being poor is a frame of mind. Being broke is only a temporary situation.
—Mike Todd

Have I earned what I have by myself?

Do I think that is important?

Do I work too hard for my money, not hard enough, or about right for me? I feel overpaid/paid about the right amount/underpaid for the work I do now because _____ .

The best thing about my financial situation is _____ .

The thing about my financial situation that worries me most or has me the most dissatisfied is _____ .

How do I think people get rich?

Am I rich?

Do I want to be rich?

How much is rich for me?

Realistically, how do I see myself in terms of my finances one year from now and five years from now?

Is my present course taking me there?

What other issues regarding my finances do I want to explore?

All prosperity begins in the mind and is dependent only upon the full use of our creative imagination.
—Ruth Ross, Ph.D.

Things I Like About My Financial Condition	*Things I Don't Like About My Financial Condition*

List as many things as possible.

*L*ife is a gamble, at terrible odds—if it was a
bet you wouldn't take it.
—Tom Stoppard

Now that you've made two lists, it's time to examine them. First of all, which is longer? Which is longer when you consider only those items that are circled (the things that are important to you)?

If the list of important things you don't like is much longer than the list of things you do like, you might then consider asking yourself whether or not you should concentrate on changing your financial outlook and goals. If the list of things you do like is much longer, you may want to concentrate instead on continuing along your current course. In either case, it's time to work on changing whichever circled items that are within your control to change.

So that's the first and most important question to ask yourself: Which items on the list of things I don't like are within my control to change? (It may help to examine the reasons these problems exist in the first place.)

P·L·A·N

What are three things I can do to change each item on the list? List everything now. Later go back and think about the consequences and repercussions of each possible action. Think then, for example, if rectifying a problem will negatively affect any of the things on the other list, the things you do like about your financial condition.

THINGS I CAN CHANGE

A.

B.

WAYS TO CHANGE THEM

A 1.

2.

3.

B 1.

2.

3.

POSSIBLE CONSEQUENCES

A 1.

2.

3.

B 1.

2.

3.

Following is a list of general and specific positive actions you may want to consider taking. Not everything on the list of suggestions will apply to you nor will they all be right for you. It is hoped, though, that the list will inspire you to come up with

your own ideas about how to help yourself, plan for the future, and improve your life. Not forgetting to weigh the risks and consequences, could you see yourself taking any of these actions?

I could take a course in investing.

I could read a book about investing.

I could start reading a business magazine.

I could pay more attention to my investments.

I could start a home budget.

I could start my own business.

I could change my business or streamline it.

I could look for work.

I could work for _____ .

I could look for different work.

I could take a training course.

I could buy a franchise.

I could make money in my spare time by _____ .

I could practice a skill.

I could develop a skill.

I could make money from a skill that I don't use.

I could make money from doing my hobby.

I could change my job.

I could ask for a raise.

I could ask for a promotion.

I could save more money by _____ .

I could spend less money on _____ .

I could invest in a _____ .

I could get a second job.

I could probably make more money than I do if I would _____ .

I could try to be less _____ .

I could try to be more _____ .

I could get insurance or more insurance.

I could try safer investments.

I could try riskier investments.

I could reduce my taxes by _____ .

I could take a course in taxes.

I could read a book about taxes.

I could save for a _____ .

I could put $ _____ into the bank each month.

I could investigate mortgages.

I could get a second mortgage.

I could get a loan for _____ .

I could pay back my loan.

I could get a credit card with a lower interest rate.

I could stop using my credit cards.

I could get a credit card.

I could make an effort to pay my credit cards each month.

I could stop spending money frivolously.

I could stop eating in restaurants so frequently.

I could bring my lunch to work.

I could balance my checkbook regularly.

I could be less generous.

I could make gifts for others.

I could use coupons when I shop.

I could look for sales.

I could put off _____ until I can afford it better.

I could vacation closer to home.

I could work overtime.

I could take up a cheaper hobby.

I could ask _____ for help.

I could plan for retirement.

I could retire when I am _____ if I would _____ .

I could seek a financial advisor.

I could ask knowledgeable friends and relatives to advise me.

I could go back to school full time.

I could take an evening course.

*Y*ou may be disappointed if you fail, but you are doomed if you don't try.
—Beverly Sills

I could work longer hours.

I could think more of the far future.

I could think more of the present and the immediate future.

I could sell my _____.

I could buy a _____.

I could start _____.

I could start _____.

I could stop _____.

I could stop _____.

I could _____.

I could _____.

I could _____.

I could _____.

I could _____.

Now it's time to . . .

A·C·T

Look at your new list and ask yourself the following questions:

Which of these things could I do or start doing today?

Which of these things take time?

Are there any first steps I can take today to achieve any of my long-term goals? (For example, if you've decided to go on a budget but don't know where to begin, today you could buy a home budget book.)

What are the general things I will try to do?

Tell yourself, I will do at least one new thing per day until I am satisfied with my financial condition. I will do everything in my power to work within my limitations. I will try to set realistic goals and will note each accomplishment. I will perceive myself as successful just for trying, and I will be gentle with myself if things do not turn out the way I expect. If I do not accomplish something I have set out to do, I will consider the possibility that I have tried to change something that is not within my power to change, and I will try to learn lessons that will help me in this and other areas of my life. I will not expect to change everything all at once but will take things one step at a time.

Things I Could Do Today: | *Things That Take Time:*

I Will Do the Following Things Today:

*D*on't look back. Something may be gaining on you.
— *Satchel Paige*

3. School

F·O·C·U·S

When people ask me, "How's school?" or "What are you studying?" this is what I say:

This is how I really feel about school and being a student:

This is how I spend a typical day:

Make two lists side by side. On the left, list all of those things about being a student in school that you like. On the right, list all of the things about school that you don't like. Think of everything, general and specific, important and trivial, but circle everything that is very important to you, because these are the things that will deserve special attention later.

Ask yourself any or all of the following questions that apply to you. If you like, jot down your answers right on the page. Then later, transfer each answer to whichever list it fits; it's possible that some things will go on both lists:

What are the worst things about being in school?

What are the best things about being in school?

Does being a student suit my personality?

Do I get enough physical exercise?

Do I feel relaxed or wound up most of the time?

Do I get enough sleep?

Do I have good study habits?

Do I study too hard, not hard enough, or about the right amount for me?

Am I satisfied with my grades?

Am I satisfied with the level of education?

Do I like my teachers?

Do I have enough, too much, or just about the right amount of leisure time?

Do I enjoy my leisure time?

Do I prefer my schoolwork or my leisure time?

Am I satisfied with my financial situation?

Do I work for wages?

Am I satisfied with that work and the income it brings?

Are there any financial considerations about being in school that are of concern to me?

Am I glad I am at this school? If not, do I feel it's working out okay?

Why am I in school or in this school?

Is there a school I would prefer to be at?

Why am I not there?

Is there a way I could transfer to it?

Am I learning what I come to school to learn?

Is it something that will be useful to me?

Would I prefer not to be in school at all?

What are my talents and skills?

Of those, which do I enjoy using the most?

Does my school or my life outside of school allow me to practice or improve those talents and skills?

What are my interests?

Do I know what's available at my school and am I making use of its resources?

Do I belong to any clubs or organizations? If so, what do I get out of my involvement in them?

What kind of work am I thinking about doing when I'm no longer in school?

Do I have a major? If so, do I see it as leading to anything for me?

Does that matter to me?

Am I satisfied with my living situation and roommate(s) or other people I live with?

Is my environment conducive to studying?

Is it easy enough for me to get to my classes?

Do I have the proper tools to study with?

Do I have any limitations that make it hard to study?

Am I satisfied with my social life?

Do I have enough time to do what's important to me?

Is drug and alcohol use prevalent at my school, and is this an issue for me in any way?

Can I pinpoint the problems in my life?

Am I under any excessive pressure?

Do I pressure myself to achieve or does my family pressure me?

Do my problems interfere with my studies?

Are there other issues about school I want to focus on?

Am I looking forward, do I dread, or am I not concerned about the day when I am out of school?

What do I hope to have gotten out of my education over the next five years?

Realistically, how do I see myself in terms of school one year from now and five years from now?

Is my present course taking me there?

What other issues regarding my school do I want to explore?

Things I Like About School	*Things I Don't Like About School*

List as many things as possible.

*S*tand firm in your refusal to remain conscious during
algebra. In real life, I assure you, there is no
such thing as algebra.
—*Fran Lebowitz*

Now that you've made two lists, it's time to examine them. First of all, which is longer? Which is longer when you consider only those items that are circled (the things that are important to you)?

If the list of important things you don't like is much longer than the list of things you do like, you might then consider asking yourself whether or not, if possible, you should consider not being a student or changing schools. If the list of things you do like is much longer, you may want to concentrate instead on improving your life as a student. In either case, it's time to work on changing whichever circled items that are within your control to change.

So that's the first and most important question to ask yourself: Which items on the list of things I don't like are within my control to change? (It may help to examine the reasons these problems exist in the first place.)

P·L·A·N

What are three things I can do to change each item on the list? List everything now. Later go back and think about the consequences and repercussions of each possible action. Think then, for example, if rectifying a problem will negatively affect any of the things on the other list, the things you do like about your work.

THINGS I CAN CHANGE

A.

B.

WAYS TO CHANGE THEM

A 1.

2.

3.

B 1.

2.

3.

POSSIBLE CONSEQUENCES

A 1.

2.

3.

B 1.

2.

3.

Following is a list of general and specific positive actions you may want to consider taking. Not everything on the list of suggestions will apply to you nor will they all be right for you. It is hoped, though, that the list will inspire you to come up with

your own ideas about how to help yourself, plan for the future, and improve your life. Not forgetting to weigh the risks and consequences, could you see yourself taking any of these actions?

I could read the school catalog.

I could save for or borrow a computer.

I could change my status from full- to part-time or vice versa.

I could sign up for work-study or get a job after school.

I could apply for financial aid.

I could research scholarship opportunities.

I could join some clubs.

I could use the gym more often.

I could try to make new friends.

I could get a new roommate.

I could do more/less with my roommate.

I could transfer to a local/distant school.

I could try to improve the quality of my leisure time.

I could move on/off campus.

I could study harder or not quite so hard.

I could plan my time better so that I don't have to stay up all night.

I could get a tutor.

I could become a tutor.

I could get a part-time job.

I could change my major.

I could become involved in the community.

I could find new ways to relax (yoga, meditation, poetry, concerts).

I could talk to certain teachers.

I could drop a course.

I could sign up for a specific class.

I could look for a new hobby.

I could prepare my résumé.

I could be nicer to certain people.

I could come home earlier.

I could stay away from drugs and alcohol.

I could get a car.

I could use my qualifications to become a _____.

I could become qualified to be a _____.

I could talk to a career counselor.

I could do library research.

I could take a leave of absence.

I could plan for the next vacation.

I could pay someone or barter with him/her to type my papers.

I could start _____.

I could start _____.

I could stop _____ .

I could stop _____ .

I could _____ .

I could _____ .

I could _____ .

I could _____ .

I could _____ .

Now it's time to . . .

A·C·T

Look at your new list and ask yourself the following questions:

Which of these things could I do or start doing today?

Which of these things take time?

Are there any first steps I can take today to achieve any of my long-term goals? (For example, if you've decided to improve your grade in chemistry, today you could read the next chapter in your textbook.)

What general things will I try to do?

Tell yourself, I will do at least one new thing per day until I am satisfied with my school life. I will do everything in my power to work within my limitations. I will try to set realistic goals and will note each accomplishment. I will perceive myself as successful just for trying, and I will be gentle with myself if things do not turn out the way I expect. If I do not accomplish something I have set out to do, I will consider the possibility that I have tried to change something that is not within my power to change, and I will try to learn lessons that will help me in this and other areas of my life. I will not expect to change everything all at once but will take things one step at a time.

Things I Could Do Today:	*Things That Take Time:*

I Will Do the Following Things Today:

E·V·A·L·U·A·T·E

I will keep a list here of all of the things I've done and the results I've achieved:

DATE	STEP TAKEN	RESULTS

*R*aise your sail one foot and you get ten feet of wind.
—Chinese proverb

V.

HERE I AM AGAIN: BUILDING ON MY EXPERIENCE UP UNTIL NOW

1. What I've Learned About What's Possible for Me:
A Checklist of Changes I've Made
2. The Pep Talk I Want to Give Myself:
Things I Still Need to Work On
3. Moving Right Along:
The Next Challenge

1. What I've Learned About What's Possible for Me: A Checklist of Changes I've Made

Look over your evaluations at the end of each part you have worked on and try to summarize: think of the best changes and plans you made, your major accomplishments, things that didn't work out so well, things you'd like to do more of, things you'd like to do in addition. Don't forget to look at the risks you took and how they worked out and any possible negative consequences that you'd like to avoid in the future.

The following are highlights of the things I've done and the results I've achieved:

HEALTH

DATE	STEP TAKEN	RESULTS

*H**alf my life is an act of revision.*
    —John Irving

FAMILY AND RELATIONSHIPS
DATE   STEP TAKEN   RESULTS

HOME AND COMMUNITY
DATE   STEP TAKEN   RESULTS

WORK AND SCHOOL
DATE   STEP TAKEN   RESULTS

OTHER
DATE   STEP TAKEN   RESULTS

I always remember an epitaph which is in the cemetery at Tombstone, Arizona. It says: "Here lies Jack Williams. He done his damnednest." I think that is the greatest epitaph a man can have—when he gives everything that is in him to do the job he has before him. That is all you can ask of him and that is what I have tried to do.
—Harry S. Truman

*W*e should be careful to get out of an experience only the wisdom that's in it—and stop there; lest we be like the cat that sits down on a hot stove-lid. She will never sit down on a hot stove-lid again—and that is well; but also she will never sit down on a cold one again.
—Mark Twain

2. The Pep Talk I Want to Give Myself: Things I Still Need to Work On

If you're having trouble getting started, begin by thumbing through this book—your book. Evaluate your progress. Are you pleased? Why? How could you do better? Read the quotes that are sprinkled throughout the book. Circle the ones that inspire you. Incorporate those sentiments into your pep talk. Be positive. Why are you terrific? List all of your best qualities. How can you be even better? If you could have anything in the world, what things would you want? What would make you feel great? How are you going to get some of those things?

Use the technique you've learned in this book to work further on those areas of your life that you have chosen to focus on or come up with some new ones.

*T*he future is something which everyone reaches at the rate of sixty minutes an hour, whatever he does, whoever he be.
—C. S. Lewis

A List of Plans I'd Like to Make and Issues I'd Like to Resolve

*T*he man who views the world at fifty the same as he
did at twenty has wasted thirty years of his life.
—*Muhammad Ali*

3. Moving Right Along: The Next Challenge

Using the techniques you've learned in this book, choose a subject of concern to you and tailor-make your own five-year plan.

FOCUS:

PLAN:

ACT:

EVALUATE:

*G*o, seeker, if you will, throughout the land. . . .
 Observe the whole of it, survey it as you might
survey a field. . . . It's your oyster—yours to open if you
will. . . . Just make yourself at home, refresh yourself, get
the feel of things, adjust your sights, and get the scale. . . .
To every man his chance—to every man, regardless of his
birth, his shining, golden opportunity—to every man the
right to live, to work, to be himself, and to become whatever thing his manhood and his vision can combine to make
him—this, seeker, is the promise of America.
 —*Thomas Wolfe*

Selected Resources

Adair, M. *Working Inside Out: Tools for Change.* Berkeley, CA.: Wingbow Press, 1984.

Avery, A. C., with Furst, E., and Hammel, D. D. *Successful Aging: A Sourcebook for Older People and Their Families.* New York: Ballantine, 1987.

Bach, G. R., and Deutsch, R. M. *Pairing: How to Achieve Genuine Intimacy.* New York: Avon, 1971.

Benson, H., with Klipper, M. Z. *The Relaxation Response.* New York: Avon, 1976.

Bergman, D. *Inner Voyager.* New York: Simon & Schuster, 1989.

Borhek, N. V. *Coming Out to Parents: A Two Way Survival Guide for Lesbians and Gay Men and Their Parents.* New York: Pilgrim Press, 1983.

Boston Women's Health Collective. *The New Our Bodies, Ourselves.* New York: Simon & Schuster, 1984.

Boston Women's Health Collective. *Ourselves and Our Children.* New York: Random House, 1978.

Brody, Jane. *Jane Brody's The New York Times Guide to Personal Health.* New York: Avon, 1983.

Bruckner-Gordon, F., Gangi, B. K., and Wallman, G. U., *Making Therapy Work.* New York: Harper & Row, 1988.

Buzan, Tony. *Use Both Sides of the Brain.* New York: Dutton, 1983.

Calgrove, N., Bloomfield, H., and McWilliams, P. *How to Survive a Loss.* New York: Bantam, 1981.

Carter, J., and Carter, R. *Making the Most of the Rest of Your Life.* New York: Random House, 1987.

Chesanow, N., and Esersky, G. L. *Please Read This for Me: How to Tell the Man You Love Things You Can't Put Into Words.* New York: Arbor/ Morrow, 1988.

Clark, D. *Loving Someone Gay.* New York: Signet, 1977.

Comfort, A. *The Joy of Sex.* New York: Pocket Books, 1987.

Cousins, N. *Anatomy of an Illness as Perceived by a Patient: Reflections on Healing and Regeneration.* New York: Bantam, 1981.

Crystal, John, and Bolles, Richard N. *What Color Is Your Parachute?* Berkeley, CA.: Ten Speed Press, Annual.

Douglas, P. H., and Pinshy, L., in cooperation with the Columbia University Health Services. *The Essential AIDS Fact Book: What You Need to Know to Protect Yourself, Your Family, All Your Loved Ones.* New York: Pocket Books, 1987.

Edenberg, M. A. *Talking with Your Aging Parent.* Boston: Shambhala, 1987.

Ehrenberg, O., and Ehrenberg, M. *The Psychotherapy Maze: A Consumer's Guide to Getting In and Out of Therapy.* New York: Simon & Schuster, 1986.

Faber, Adele, and Mazlish, E. *Siblings Without Rivalry.* New York: Avon, 1988.

Fonda, J., with McCarthy, M. *Woman Coming of Age.* New York: Simon & Schuster, 1984.

Fraiberg, S. *The Magic Years: Understanding and Handling the Problems of Early Childhood.* New York: Scribners, 1959.

Freud, S. *The Interpretation of Dreams.* New York: Avon, 1965.

Garner, Alan. *Conversationally Speaking: Tested New Ways to Increase Your Personal and Social Effectiveness.* New York: McGraw-Hill, 1981.

Gordon, T. *Parent Effectiveness Training.* New York: Wyden, 1970.

Greene, J., and Lewis, D. *Know Your Own Mind.* New York: Rawson, 1983.

Hale, G., ed. *The Source Book for the Disabled.* New York: Bantam, 1981.

Harragan, Betty Lehan. *Games Mother Never Taught You: Corporate Gamesmanship for Women.* New York: Warner Books, 1977.

Hay, L. *You Can Heal Your Life.* Hay House, 1984.

Irish, Richard K. *Go Hire Yourself an Employer.* New York: Doubleday/ Anchor, 1987.

Kohl, S., and Bregman, A. M. *Have a Love Affair With Your Husband.* New York: St. Martin's, 1987.

Kübler-Ross, E. *On Death and Dying.* New York: Macmillan, 1969.

Kushner, H. *When Bad Things Happen to Good People.* New York: Avon, 1984.

LeBoeuf, Michael. *Imagineering.* New York: Berkley Books, 1980.

LeBoeuf, Michael. *Working Smart.* New York: Warner Books, 1979.

Ledray, L. *Recovering from Rape.* New York: Holt, 1986.

Lerner, Harriet G. *Dance of Intimacy*. New York: Harper & Row, 1988.

Marlin, E. *Hope: New Choices and Recovery Strategies for Adult Children of Alcoholics*. New York: Harper & Row, 1987.

Orbach, S. *Fat Is a Feminist Issue*. New York: Berkley, 1982.

Papolos, D. F., and Papolos, J. *Overcoming Depression*. New York: Harper & Row, 1987.

Papp, P. *The Process of Change*. New York: Guilford Press, 1983.

Peck, Scott. *The Road Less Traveled*. New York: Touchstone, 1985.

Pogrebin, L. C. *Among Friends: Who We Like, Why We Like Them, and What We Do with Them*. New York: McGraw-Hill, 1987.

Rainer, T. *The New Diary: How to Use a Journal for Self-Guidance and Expanded Creativity*. Los Angeles: J. P. Tarcher, 1978.

Ram Dass. *Journey of Awakening: A Meditator's Guidebook*. New York: Bantam Books, 1978.

Ronco, William. *Jobs: How People Create Their Own*. Boston: Beacon Press, 1977.

Sangrey, Dawn. *Wifestyles: Women Talk About Marriage*. New York: Delacorte Press, 1983.

Satir, Virginia. *Peoplemaking*. Palo Alto, CA.: Science & Behavior Books, 1972.

Scarf, M. *Intimate Partners: Patterns in Love and Marriage*. New York: Random House, 1987.

Sheehy, Gail. *Passages: Predictable Crises of Adult Life*. New York: E. P. Dutton, 1976.

Sher, B., with Gottlieb, A. *Wishcraft: How to Get What You Really Want*, New York: Ballantine, 1979.

Siegel, B. S. *Love, Medicine, and Miracles*. New York: Harper & Row, 1986.

Siegel, M., Brisman, J., and Weinshel, M. *Surviving an Eating Disorder*. New York: Harper & Row, 1987.

Simon, S. *Getting Unstuck*, New York: Warner, 1988.

Smith, Manuel J. *When I Say No I Feel Guilty*. New York: Bantam Books, 1975.

Soltanoff, J. S. *Natural Healing*. New York: Warner, 1988.

Viorst, Judith. *Necessary Losses: The Loves, Illusions, Dependencies, and Impossible Expectations*. New York: Ballantine, 1986.

Weiner, F. *No Apologies: A Guide to Living with a Disability*. New York: St. Martin's, 1986.

Winston, S. *Getting Organized*. New York: Norton, 1978.